Cam Hillier was in the foyer talking to Molly when Liz walked in. He had his back to her, but he saw Molly's eyes widen as she looked past him and he swung round.

For a moment he didn't recognise Liz. Then she saw him do a double-take and he whistled softly. It was something she would have found extremely satisfying except for one thing. He also allowed his blue gaze to drift down her body, to linger on her legs. Then he looked back into her eyes in the way that men let women know they were being summed up as bed partners.

To her annoyance, that pointed, slow drift of assessment up and down her body caused her those sensations she'd experienced when she'd tripped on the pavement: accelerated breathing, a rush through her senses, an awareness of how tall and beautifully made he was.

Only thanks to her lingering resentment did she manage not to blush. She even tilted her chin at him instead.

'I see,' he said gravely. 'I was not to know you could look like this—stunning, in other words. Nor was I to know that you could conjure *haute couture* clothes out of thin air.' He studied her jacket for a moment, then looked into her eyes.

Lindsay Armstrong was born in South Africa, but now lives in Australia with her New Zealand-born husband and their five children. They have lived in nearly every state of Australia, and have tried their hand at some unusual—for them—occupations, such as farming and horse-training—all grist to the mill for a writer! Lindsay started writing romances when their youngest child began school and she was left feeling at a loose end. She is still doing it and loving it.

Recent titles by the same author:

THE SOCIALITE AND THE CATTLE KING
ONE-NIGHT PREGNANCY
THE BILLIONAIRE BOSS'S INNOCENT BRIDE
FROM WAIF TO HIS WIFE
THE RICH MAN'S VIRGIN

THE GIRL HE NEVER NOTICED

BY
LINDSAY ARMSTRONG

MILLS
BOON

First published in Great Britain 2011
by Mills & Boon, an imprint of Harlequin (UK) Limited,
Eton House, 18-24 Paradise Road, Richmond, Surrey TW9 1SR

© Lindsay Armstrong 2011

ISBN: 978 0 263 22026 1

Harlequin (UK) policy is to use papers that are natural, renewable
and recyclable products and made from wood grown in sustainable
forests. The logging and manufacturing process conform to the
legal environmental regulations of the country of origin.

Printed and bound in Great Britain
by CPI Antony Rowe, Chippenham, Wiltshire

THE GIRL HE
NEVER NOTICED

CHAPTER ONE

'MISS MONTROSE,' Cameron Hillier said, 'where the hell is my date?'

Liz Montrose raised her eyebrows. 'I have no idea, Mr Hillier. How should I?'

'Because it's your job—you're my diary secretary, aren't you?'

Liz stared at Cam Hillier, as he was known, with her nostrils slightly pinched. She didn't know him well. She'd only been in this position for a week and a half, and only because an agency had supplied her to fill the gap created by his regular diary secretary's illness. But even that short time had been long enough to discover that he could be difficult, demanding and arrogant.

What was she supposed to do about the apparent non-appearance of his date, though?

She looked around a little wildly. They were in the outer office—his secretary Molly Swanson's domain— and Molly, heaven bless her, Liz thought, was holding a phone receiver out to her and making gestures behind his back.

'Uh, I'll just check,' Liz said to her boss.

He shrugged and walked back into his office.

'What's her name?' Liz whispered to Molly as she took the phone.

'Portia Pengelly.'

Liz grimaced, then frowned. 'Not the model and TV star?'

Molly nodded at the same time as someone answered the phone.

'Uh—Miss Pengelly?' Liz said down the line and, on receiving confirmation, went on, 'Miss Pengelly, I'm calling on behalf of Mr Hillier, Mr Cameron Hillier...'

Two minutes later she handed the receiver back to Molly, her face a study of someone caught between laughter and disaster.

'What?' Molly queried.

'She'd rather go out with a two-timing snake! How can I tell him that?'

Cam Hillier's office was minimalist: a thick green carpet, ivory slatted blinds at the windows, a broad oak desk with a green leather chair behind it and two smaller ones in front of it. Liz thought it was uncluttered and restful, although the art on the walls reflected two of the very different and not necessarily restful enterprises that had made him a multi-millionaire—horses and a fishing fleet.

There were silver-framed paintings of stallions, mares and foals. There were seascapes with trawlers in them—trawlers with their nets out and flocks of seagulls around them.

Liz had studied these pictures in her boss's absence and

discovered a curious and common theme: Shakespeare. The three stallions portrayed were called Hamlet, Prospero and Othello. The trawlers were named *Miss Miranda*, *Juliet's Joy*, *As You Like It*, *Cordelia's Catch* and so on.

She would, she felt, like to know where the Shakespeare theme came from. But the thing was you did not take Cam Hillier lightly or engage in idle chit-chat with him. She'd been made aware of this before she'd laid eyes on him. The employment agency she worked for had warned her that he was an extremely high-powered businessman and not easy to handle, so if she had any reservations about how to cope with a man like that she should not even consider the position. They'd also warned her that 'diary secretary' could cover a multitude of sins.

But she'd coped with a variety of high-powered businessmen before; in fact she seemed to have a gift for it. Though, it crossed her mind that she'd never had to tell any of those men that the woman in their life would rather consort with a snake...

And there was another difference with Cam Hillier. He was young—early thirties at the most—he was extremely fit, and he was—well, she'd heard it said by his female accountant: 'In an indefinable way he's as sexy as hell.'

What was so indefinable about it? she'd wondered at the time. He was tall, lean and rangy, with broad shoulders. He had thick dark hair, and deep, brooding blue eyes in not a precisely handsome face, true, but those eyes alone could send a shiver down your spine as they summed you up.

In fact, to her annoyance, Liz had to admit that she was not immune to Cam Hillier's powerfully masculine presence. Nor could she persuade her mind to discard the cameo-like memory that had brought this home to her...

It was a hot Sydney day as they walked side by side down a crowded pavement to a meeting. They were walking because it was only two blocks from his offices to their destination. The traffic was roaring past, the tall buildings of the CBD were creating a canyon-like effect and the sidewalk was crowded when Liz caught her heel on an uneven paver.

She staggered, and would have fallen, but he grabbed her and held her with his hands on her shoulders until she regained her balance.

'Th-thanks,' she stammered.

'OK?' He looked down at her with an eyebrow lifted.

'Fine,' she lied. Because she was anything but fine. Out of nowhere she was deeply affected by the feel of his hands on her, deeply affected by his closeness, by how tall he was, how wide his shoulders were, how thick his dark hair was.

Above all, she was stunned by the unfurling sensations that ran through her body under the impact of being so close to Cam Hillier.

She did have the presence of mind to lower her lashes swiftly so he couldn't read her eyes; she would have been mortified if she'd blushed or given any other in-dication of her disarray.

He dropped his hands and they walked on.

Since that day Liz had been particularly careful in her boss's presence not to trip or do anything that could trigger those sensations again. If Cam Hillier had noticed anything he'd given no sign of it—which, of course, had been helpful. Not so helpful was the tiny voice from somewhere inside her that didn't appreciate her having the status of a robot where he was concerned.

She'd been shocked when that thought had surfaced. She'd told herself she'd have hated him if he'd acted in any way outside the employer/employee range; she couldn't believe she was even thinking it!

And finally she'd filed the incident away under the label of 'momentary aberration', even though she couldn't quite command herself to banish it entirely.

But somewhat to her surprise—considering the conflicting emotions she was subject to, considering the fact that although Cam Hillier could be a maddening boss he had a crooked grin that was quite a revelation—she'd managed to cope with the job with her usual savoir-faire for the most part.

He wasn't smiling now as he looked up from the papers he was studying and raised an eyebrow at her.

'Miss Pengelly…' Liz began, and swallowed. *Miss Pengelly regrets?* In all honesty she couldn't say that. *Miss Pengelly sends her regards?* Portia certainly hadn't done that! 'Uh—she's not coming. Miss Pengelly isn't,' she added, in case there was any misunderstanding.

Cam Hillier twitched his eyebrows together and swore under his breath. 'Just like that?' he shot at Liz.

'Er—more or less.' Liz felt her cheeks warm a little.

Cam studied her keenly, then that crooked grin played across his lips and was gone almost before it had begun. 'I see,' he said gravely. 'I'm sorry if you were embarrassed, but the thing is—you'll have to come in her place.'

'I certainly will not!' It was out before Liz could stop herself.

'Why not? It's only a cocktail party.'

Liz breathed unevenly. 'Precisely. Why can't you go on your own?'

'I don't like going to parties on my own. I tend to get mobbed. Portia,' he said with some exasperation, 'was brilliant at deflecting unwanted advances. They took one look at her and I guess—' he shrugged '—felt the competition was just too great.'

Liz blinked. 'Is that all she was...?' She tailed off and gestured, as if to say *strike that*... 'Look here, Mr Hillier,' she said instead, 'if your diary secretary—the one I'm replacing—were here, you wouldn't be able to take *him* along to ward off the...unwanted advances.'

'True,' he agreed. 'But Roger would have been able to find me someone.'

Liz compressed her lips as she thought with distaste, *rent-an-escort*? 'Well, I can't do that either,' she said tartly, and was struck by another line of defence. 'And I certainly don't have Portia Pengelly's...er...powers of repelling boarders.'

Cam Hillier got up and strolled round his desk. 'Oh, I

don't know about that.' He sat on the corner of the desk and studied her—particularly her scraped-back hair and her horn-rimmed glasses. 'You're very fair, aren't you?' he murmured.

'What's that got to do with it?' Liz enquired tartly, and added as she looked down at her elegant but essentially plain ivory linen dress, 'Anyway, I'm not dressed for a party!'

He shrugged. 'You'll do. In fact, those light blue eyes, that fair hair and the severe outfit give you quite an "Ice Queen" aura. Just as effective in its own way as Portia, I'd say.'

Liz felt herself literally swell with anger, and had to take some deep breaths. But almost immediately her desire to slap his face and walk out was tempered by the thought that she was to be very well paid for the month she'd agreed to work for him. And also tempered by the thought that walking out—not to mention striking him—would place a question mark if not a huge black mark against her record with the employment agency...

He watched and waited attentively.

She muttered something under her breath and said audibly, but coolly, 'I'll come. But purely on an employer/employee basis—and I'll need a few minutes to freshen up.'

What she saw in his eyes then—a wicked little glint of amusement—did not improve her mood, but he stood up and said only, 'Thank you, Miss Montrose. I appreciate this gesture. I'll meet you in the foyer in fifteen minutes.'

* * *

Liz washed her face and hands in the staff bathroom—a symphony of mottled black marble and wide, well-lit mirrors. She was still simmering with annoyance, and not only that. She was seriously offended, she discovered—and dying to bite back!

She stared at herself in the mirror. It was on purpose that she dressed formally but plainly for work, but it was not how she always dressed. She happened to have a mother who was a brilliant dressmaker. And the little ivory dress she wore happened to have a silk jacket that went with it. Moreover, she'd picked up the jacket from the dry cleaner's during her lunch hour, and it had been hanging since then, in its plastic shroud, on the back of her office door. It was now hanging on the back of the bathroom door.

She stared at it, then lifted it down, pulled off the plastic and slipped it on. It had wide shoulders, a round neck, a narrow waist and flared slightly over her hips. She pushed the long fitted sleeves up, as the fashion of the moment dictated, but the impact of it came as much from the material as the style—a shadowy leopard skin pattern in blue, black and silver. It was unusual and stunning.

She smiled faintly at the difference it made to her—a bit like Joseph's amazing coloured coat, she thought wryly. Because her image now was much closer to that of a cocktail-party-goer rather than an office girl. Well, almost, she temporised, and slipped the jacket off—only to hesitate for another moment as she hung it up carefully.

Then she made up her mind.

She reached up and pulled the pins out of hair. It tumbled to just above her shoulders in a fair, blunt-cut curtain. She took off her glasses and reached into her purse for her contact lenses. She applied them delicately from the pad of her forefinger. Then she got out her little make-up purse and inspected the contents—she only used the minimum during the day, so she didn't have a lot to work with, but there was eyeshadow and mascara and some lip gloss.

She went to work on her eyes and again, as she stood back to study her image, the difference was quite startling. She sprayed on some perfume, brushed her hair, then tossed her head to give it a slightly tousled look and slipped the jacket on again, doing it up with its concealed hooks and eyes. Her shoes, fortunately, were pewter-grey suede and went with the jacket perfectly.

She stood back one last time and was pleased with what she saw. But she stopped and frowned suddenly.

Did she look like an ice queen? If only he knew...

Cam Hillier was in the foyer talking to Molly when Liz walked in. He had his back to her, but he saw Molly's eyes widen as she looked past him and he swung round.

For a moment he didn't recognise Liz. Then she saw him do a double-take and he whistled softly. It was something she would have found extremely satisfying except for one thing. He also allowed his blue gaze to drift down her body, to linger on her legs, and then he looked back into her eyes in the way that men let women know they were being summed up as bed partners.

To her annoyance that pointed, slow drift of assessment up and down her body reignited those sensations she'd experienced when she'd tripped on the pavement: accelerated breathing, a rush through her senses, an awareness of how tall and beautifully made he was.

Only thanks to her lingering resentment did she manage not to blush. She even tilted her chin at him instead.

'I see,' he said gravely. He shoved his hands in his trouser pockets before adding equally gravely, although she didn't for a moment imagine it was genuine. 'I'm sorry if I offended you, Miss Montrose. I was not to know you could look like this—stunning, in other words. Nor was I to know that you could conjure *haute couture* clothes out of thin air.' He studied her jacket for a moment, then looked into her eyes. 'OK. Let's go.'

They reached the cocktail party venue in record time. This was partly due to the power and manoeuvrability of his car, a graphite-blue Aston Martin, and partly due to his skill as a driver and his knowledge of the back streets so he'd been able to avoid the after-work Sydney traffic.

Liz had refused to clutch the armrest, or demonstrate any form of nerves, but she did say when they pulled up and he killed the motor, 'I think you missed your calling, Mr Hillier. You should be driving Formula One cars.'

'I did. In my misspent youth,' he replied easily. 'It got a bit boring.'

'Well, I couldn't call that drive boring. But you can't park here, can you?'

He'd pulled up in the driveway of the house next door to what she could see was a mansion behind a high wall that was lit up like a birthday cake and obviously the party venue.

'It's not a problem,' he murmured.

'But what if the owner wants to get in or out?' she queried.

'The owner is out,' he replied.

Liz shrugged and surveyed the scene again.

She knew they were in Bellevue Hill, one of Sydney's classiest suburbs, and she knew she was in for a classy event. None of it appealed to her in the slightest.

'All right.' She reached for the door handle. 'Shall we get this over and done with?'

'Just a moment,' Cam Hillier said dryly. 'I've acknowledged that I may have offended you—I've apologised. And you, with this stunning metamorphosis, have clearly had the last laugh. Is there any reason, therefore, for you to look so disapproving? Like a minder—or a governess.'

Liz flushed faintly and was struck speechless.

'What exactly do you disapprove of?' he queried.

Liz found her tongue. 'If you really want to know—'

'I do,' he broke in to assure her.

She opened her mouth, then bit her lip. 'Nothing. It's not my place to approve or otherwise. There.' She widened her eyes, straightened her spine and squared her shoulders, slipping her hair delicately behind her ears. Lastly she did some facial gymnastics, and then turned to him. 'How's that?'

Cam Hillier stared at her expressionlessly for a long moment and a curious thing happened. In the close confines of the car it wasn't disapproval that threaded through the air between them, but an awareness of each other.

Liz found herself conscious again of the width of his shoulders beneath the jacket of his charcoal suit, worn with a green shirt and a darker green tie. She was aware of the little lines beside his mouth and that clever, brooding dark blue gaze.

Not only that, but she seemed to be more sensitive to textures—such as the beautiful quality fabric of his suit and the rich leather of the car's upholstery.

And she was very aware of the way he was watching her… A physical summing up again, that brought her out in little goosebumps—because they were so close it was impossible, she suddenly found, not to imagine his arms around her, his hand in her hair, his mouth on hers.

She turned away abruptly.

He said nothing but opened his door. Liz did the same and got out without his assistance.

Although Liz had been fully aware she was in for a classy event, what she saw as she stepped through the front door of the Bellevue Hill home almost took her breath away. A broad stone-flagged passage led to the first of three descending terraces and a magnificent view of Sydney Harbour in the last of the daylight. Flaming braziers lit the terraces, pottery urns were laden with exotic flowering shrubs, and on the third and lowest terrace an aquamarine pool appeared to flow over the edge.

There were a lot of guests already assembled—an animated throng—the women making a bouquet of colours as well. In a corner of the middle terrace an energetic band was making African music with a mesmerising rhythm and the soft but fascinating throb of drums.

A dinner-suited waiter wearing white gloves was at their side immediately, offering champagne.

Liz was about to decline, but Cam simply put a glass in her hand. No sooner had he done so than their hostess descended on them.

She was a tall, striking woman, wearing a rose-pink caftan and a quantity of gold and diamond jewellery. Her silver hair was streaked with pink.

'My dear Cam,' she enthused as she came up to them, 'I thought you weren't coming!' She turned to Liz and her eyebrows shot up. 'But who is this?'

'This, Narelle, is Liz Montrose. Liz, may I introduce you to Narelle Hastings?'

Liz extended her hand and murmured, 'How do you do?'

'Very well, my dear, very well,' Narelle Hastings replied as she summed Liz up speedily and expertly, taking in not only her fair looks but her stylish outfit. 'So you've supplanted Portia?'

'Not at all,' Cam Hillier responded. 'Portia has had second thoughts about me, and since Liz is replacing

Roger who is off sick at the moment, I press-ganged her into coming rather than being partnerless. That's all.'

'Darling,' Narelle said fondly to him, 'call it what you will, but don't expect me to believe it gospel and verse.' She turned to Liz. 'You're far too lovely to be just a secretary, my dear, and in his own way Cam's not bad either. It is what makes the world go round. But anyway—' she turned back to Cam '—how's Archie?'

'A nervous wreck. Wenonah's puppies are due any day.'

Narelle Hastings chuckled. 'Give him my love. Oh! Excuse me! Some more latecomers. And don't forget,' she said to Liz, 'life wasn't meant to be all work and no play, so enjoy yourself with Cam while you can!' And she wandered off.

'Don't tell me how to look,' Liz warned him.

'Wouldn't dream of it. Uh—Narelle can be a little eccentric.'

'Even so, I knew this wasn't a good idea,' she added darkly.

He studied her, then shrugged. 'I don't see it as a matter of great importance.'

Liz glanced sideways at him, as if to say *you wouldn't*! But that was a mistake, because she was suddenly conscious again of just how dangerously attractive Cameron Hillier was. Tall and dark, with that fine-tuned physique, he effortlessly drew the eyes of many of the women around them. Was it so far off the mark to imagine him being mobbed? No, that was ridiculous…

'It's not your reputation that's at stake,' she retorted finally. 'That was probably…' She paused.

'Ruined years ago?' he suggested.

Liz grimaced and looked away, thinking again, belatedly, of black marks on her record. *Did not actually come to blows with temporary employer, but did insult him by suggesting he had a questionable reputation...*

'This place is quite amazing,' she said, switching to a conversational tone, and she took a sip of champagne. 'Is the party in aid of any special event?'

Cam Hillier raised his eyebrows in some surprise at this change of pace on her part, then looked amused. 'Uh—probably not. Narelle never needs an excuse to throw a party. She's a pillar of the social scene.'

'How...interesting,' Liz said politely.

'You don't agree with holding a party just for the sake of it?' he queried.

'Did I say that? If you can afford it—' She broke off and shrugged.

'You didn't say it, but I got the feeling you were thinking it. By the way, she happens to be my great-aunt.'

Liz looked rueful and took another sip of champagne. 'Thanks.'

He looked a question at her.

'For telling me that. I...sometimes I have a problem with...with speaking my mind,' she admitted. 'But I would never say anything less than complimentary about someone's great-aunt.'

This time Cam Hillier did more than flash that crooked grin; he laughed.

'What's funny about that?'

'I'm not sure,' he returned, still looking amused. 'Confirmation of what I suspected? That you can be outspoken to a fault. Or the fact that you regard great-aunts as somehow sacred?'

Liz grimaced. 'I guess it did sound a bit odd, but you know what I mean. In general I don't like to get personal.'

He looked sceptical, but chose not to explain why. He said, 'Narelle can look after herself better than most. But how come you appear to handle a position that requires great diplomacy with ease when you have a problem with outspokenness?'

'Yes, well, it's been a bit of a mystery to me at times,' she conceded. 'Although I have been told it can be quite refreshing. But of course I do try to rein it in.'

'Not with me, though?' he suggested.

Liz studied her glass and took another sip. 'To be honest, Mr Hillier, I've never before been told to pass on the message that my employer's...um...date would rather consort with a two-timing snake than go to a party with him.'

Cam Hillier whistled softly. 'She must have been steamed up about something!'

'Yes—*you*. Then there was your own assertion that to go to a party alone would leave you open to being mobbed by women—I had a bit of difficulty with that—'

'It's my money,' he broke in.

'Uh-huh? Like your great-aunt, I won't take that one as gospel and verse either,' Liz said with considerable irony, and flinched as a flashlight went off. 'Add to that the distinct possibility that we could be now tagged as an item, and throw into the mix that death-defying drive

through the back streets of Sydney, is it any wonder I'm
having trouble holding my tongue?'

'Probably not,' he conceded. 'Would you like to leave
the job forthwith?'

'Ah,' Liz said, and studied her glass, a little surprised
to see that it was half empty, before raising her blue eyes
to his. 'Actually, no. I need the money. So if we could
just get back to office hours, and the more usual kind
of insanity that goes with a diary secretary's position,
I'd appreciate it.'

He considered for a moment. 'How old are you, and
how did you get this job—with the agency, I mean?'

'I'm twenty-four, and I have a degree in Business
Management. I topped the class, which you may find
hard to believe—but it's true.'

He narrowed his gaze. 'I don't. I realised you were
as bright as a tack from the way you handled yourself
in the first few hours of our relationship—our *working*
relationship,' he said as she looked set to take issue with
him.

'Oh?' Liz looked surprised. 'How so?'

'Remember the Fortune proposal—the seafood mar-
keting one? I virtually tossed it in your lap the first day,
because it was incomplete, and told you to fix it?'

Liz nodded. 'I do,' she said dryly.

He smiled. 'Throwing you in at the deep end and
not what you were employed for anyway? Possibly. But
I saw you study it, and then I happened to hear you on
the phone to Fortune with your summation of it and what
needed to be done to fix it. I was impressed.'

Liz took another sip of champagne. 'Well, thanks.'

'And Molly tells me you're a bit of an IT whiz.'

'Not really—but I do like computers and software,' she responded.

'It does lead me to wonder why you're temping rather than carving out a career for yourself,' he said meditatively.

Liz looked around.

A few couples had started to dance, and she was suddenly consumed by a desire to be free to do what she liked—which at this moment was to surrender herself to the African beat, the call of the drums and the wild. To be free of problems... To have a partner to dance with, to talk to, to share things with. Someone to help her lighten the load she was carrying.

Someone to help her live a bit. It was so long since she'd danced—so long since she'd let her hair down, so to speak—she'd forgotten what it was like...

As if drawn by a magnet her gaze came back to her escort, to find him looking down at her with a faint frown in his eyes and also an unspoken question. For one amazed moment she thought he was going to ask her to dance with him. That was followed by another amazed moment as she pictured herself moving into his arms and letting her body sway to the music.

Had he guessed which way her thoughts were heading? And if so, how? she wondered. Had there been a link forged between them now that he'd noticed her as a woman and not a robot—a mental link as well as a physical one?

She looked away as a tremor of alarm ran through her. She didn't want to be linked to a man, did she? She didn't want to go through that again. She was mad to have allowed Cam Hillier to taunt her into showing him she wasn't just a stick of office furniture…

She said the first thing that came to mind to break any mental link… 'Who's Archie?'

'My nephew.'

'He sounds like an animal lover.'

'He is.'

Liz waited for a moment, but it became obvious Cam Hillier was not prepared to be more forthcoming on the subject of his nephew.

Liz lifted her shoulders and looked out over the crowd.

Then her gaze sharpened, and widened, as she focused on a tall figure across the terrace. A man—a man who had once meant the world to her.

She turned away abruptly and handed her glass to her boss. 'Forgive me,' she said hurriedly, 'but I need—I need to find the powder room.' And she turned on her heel and walked inside.

How she came to get lost in Narelle Hastings' mansion she was never quite sure. She did find a powder room, and spent a useless ten minutes trying to calm herself down, but for the rest of it her inner turmoil must have been so great she'd been unable to think straight.

She came out of the powder room determined to make a discreet exit from the house, the party, Cam Hillier, the lot—only to see Narelle farewelling several guests. She did a quick about-turn and went through several doorways to find herself in the kitchen. Fortunately it was empty of staff, but she knew that could only be a very temporary state of affairs.

Never mind, she told herself. She'd leave by the back door!

The back door at first yielded a promising prospect— a service courtyard, a high wall with a gate in it.

Excellent! Except when she got to it, it was to find the gate locked.

She drew a frustrated, trembling breath as it occurred to her how acutely embarrassing this could turn out to be. How on earth would she explain it to Cameron Hillier—not to mention his great-aunt, whose house she appeared to be wandering through at will?

She gazed at the back door, and as she did so she heard voices coming from within. She doubted she had the nerve to brave the kitchen again. She turned away and studied her options. No good trying to get over the wall that fronted the street—she'd be bound to bump into someone. But the house next door, also behind the wall, was the one whose driveway Cam had parked in—the one whose owner was out, according to him. He must know them and know they were away to make that assertion, she reasoned. It certainly made that wall a better bet.

She dredged her memory and recalled that the driveway had gates that could possibly be locked too—and this adjacent wall was inside those gates. But hang on! Further along the pavement, hadn't there been a pedestrian gate? No—just a gateway. Yes! So all she had to do was climb over the wall…How the hell was she going to do that, though?

She tensed as the back door opened, and slipped into some shadows as a kitchen hand emerged and deposited a load of garbage into a green wheelie bin and slammed it shut. He didn't see her and went back inside, closing the door, but his use of the wheelie bin gave her an idea. She could push it against the wall, hoist herself onto it and slip over it to the house next door.

As with just about everything that had happened to her on this never-ending day, it wasn't a perfect plan.

Firstly, just as she was about to emerge from the shadows and move the bin to the wall, more kitchen hands emerged with loads of garbage. This led her to reconsider things.

What if she did manage to get over the wall and someone came out to find the bin in a different position? But she couldn't skulk around this service courtyard for much longer. A glance at her watch told her she'd already been there for twenty minutes.

She was biting her lip and clenching her fists in a bid to keep calm, almost certain she would have to go through the kitchen again, when something decided the matter for her.

She heard a male voice from the kitchen, calling out that he was locking the back door. She even heard the key turn.

She closed her eyes briefly, then sprinted to the bin, shoved it up against the wall, took her shoes off and threw them over. She looped her purse over her shoulder and, hitching up her dress, climbed onto the bin. Going over from Narelle's side was easy, thanks to the height of the wheelie bin. Getting down the other side was not so easy. She had to hang onto the coping and try to guess what the shortfall was.

It was only about a foot, but she lost her balance as she dropped to the ground, and fell over. She was picking herself up and examining her torn tights and a graze on her knee when the driveway gates, with the sound of a car motor behind them, began to open inwards.

She straightened up and stared with fatal fascination at a pair of headlights as a long, low, sleek car nosed through the gates and stopped abreast of her.

The driver's window was on her side, and it lowered soundlessly. She bent her head, and as her gaze clashed with the man behind the wheel things clicked into place for her…

'Oh, I see,' she said bitterly. '*You* own this place. That's how you knew it was safe to park in the driveway!'

'Got it in two, Liz,' Cam Hillier agreed from inside his graphite-blue Aston Martin. 'But what the devil *you* think you're doing is a mystery to me.'

CHAPTER TWO

'WHO IS HE?'

The question hung in the air as Liz looked around.

She was ensconced on a comfortable cinnamon velvet-covered settee. Across a broad wooden coffee table with a priceless-looking jade bonsai tree on it was a fireplace flanked by wooden-framed French doors. Above the fireplace hung what she suspected was an original Heidelberg School painting, a lovely impressionist pastoral scene that was unmistakably Australian. Tom Roberts? she wondered.

There were two matching armchairs, and some lovely pieces of furniture scattered on the polished wooden floors. The windows looked out over a floodlit scene— an elegant pool with a fountain, tall cypress pines, and beyond the lights of Sydney Harbour.

Not as spectacular as his great-aunt's residence, Cam Hillier's house was nevertheless stylish and very expensive—worth how many millions Liz couldn't even begin to think.

Its owner was seated in an armchair across from her.

He'd shrugged off his jacket, pulled off his tie and

opened the top buttons of his shirt. He'd also poured them each a brandy.

As for Liz, she'd cleaned herself up as best she could in a guest bathroom. She'd removed her torn tights, bathed her knee and applied a plaster to it. She'd washed her face and hands but not reapplied any make-up. It had hardly seemed appropriate when she had a rip in her dress, a streak of dirt on her jacket and was shoeless.

She'd been unable to find one shoe in the driveway—until they'd discovered it in a tub of water the gardener was apparently soaking a root-bound plant in.

So far, the only explanation she'd offered was that she'd seen someone at the party she'd had no desire to meet, so she'd tried to make a quick getaway that had gone horribly wrong.

She took a sip of her brandy, and felt a little better as its warmth slipped down.

She eyed Cameron Hillier and had to acknowledge that he was equally impressive lying back in an armchair, in his shirtsleeves and with his thick dark hair ruffled, as he'd been at his great-aunt's party. On top of that those fascinating, brooding blue eyes appeared to be looking right through her…

'He?' she answered at last. 'What makes you think—?'

'Come on, Liz,' he said roughly. 'If this story is true at all, I can't imagine a woman provoking that kind of reaction! Anyway, I saw you fix your gaze on some guy, then go quite pale and still before you…decamped. Causing *me* no little discomfort, incidentally,' he added dryly.

Her eyes widened. 'Did you get mobbed?'

He looked daggers at her for a moment. 'No. But I did get Narelle to search the powder rooms when I realised how long you'd been gone. She was,' he said bitterly, 'riveted.'

'And then?'

He shrugged. 'There seemed to be no sign of you, so we finally assumed you'd called a taxi and left.'

'Meanwhile I was lurking around in the service courtyard,' Liz said with a sigh. 'All right, it *was* a he. We...we were an item once, but it didn't work out and I just—I just didn't want to have to—to face him,' she said rather jaggedly.

Cam Hillier frowned. 'Fair enough,' he said slowly. 'But why not tell me and simply walk out through the front door?'

Liz bit her lip and took another sip of brandy. 'I got a bit of a shock—I felt a little overwrought,' she confessed.

'A little?' he marvelled. 'I would say more like hysterical—and that doesn't make sense. You laid yourself open to Narelle suspecting you of casing the joint. So could I, come to that. One or the other or both of us might have called the police. Plus,' he added pithily, 'I wouldn't have taken you for a hysterical type.'

Ah, but you don't know the circumstances, Liz thought, and took another fortifying sip of brandy.

'Affairs of the heart are...can be different,' she said quietly. 'You can be the essence of calm at other times, but—' She stopped and gestured, but she didn't look at him because she sounded lame even to her own ears.

He surprised her. 'So,' he said slowly, and with a considering look, 'not such an Ice Queen after all, Ms Montrose?'

Liz didn't reply.

He frowned. 'I've just remembered something. You're a single mother, aren't you?'

Liz looked up at that, her eyes suddenly as cool as ice.

He waved an impatient hand. 'I'm not being critical, but it's just occurred to me that's why you're temping.'

'Yes,' she said, and relaxed a little.

'Tell me about it.'

She cradled her glass in both hands for a moment, and, as always happened to her when she thought of the miracle in her life, some warmth flowed through her. 'She's nearly four, her name's Scout, and she's a—a living doll.' She couldn't help the smile in her voice.

'Who looks after her when you're working?'

'My mother. We live together. My father's dead.'

'It works well?' He raised an eyebrow.

'It works well,' Liz agreed. 'Scout loves my mother, and Mum…' She looked rueful. 'Well, she sometimes needs looking after, too. She can be a touch eccentric.' She sobered. 'It can be a bit of a battle at times, but we get by.'

'And Scout's father?'

Liz was jolted out of her warm place. Her expression tightened as she swallowed and took hold of herself. 'Mr Hillier, that's really none of your business.'

He studied her thoughtfully, thinking that the change

in her was quite remarkable. Obviously Scout's father was a sore point.

He grimaced, but said, 'Miss Montrose, the way you were climbing over my wall, the way you apparently roamed around my great-aunt's house *is* my business. There are a lot of valuables in both.' His blue eyes were narrowed and sharp as he stared at her. 'And I don't think I'm getting a good enough explanation for it.'

'I—I don't understand what you mean. I had no idea this was your house. I had no idea I'd be going to your great-aunt's house this evening,' she said with growing passion. 'Only an idiot would on the spur of the moment decide to rob you both!'

'Or a single mother in financial difficulties?'

He waited, then said when she didn't seem able to frame a response, 'A single mother with a very expensive taste in clothes, by the look of it.'

Liz closed her eyes and berated herself inwardly for having been such a fool. 'They aren't expensive. My mother makes them. All right!' she said suddenly, and tossed her head as she saw the disbelief in his eyes. 'It was Scout's father I saw at the party. That's what threw me into such a state. I haven't spoken to him or laid eyes on him for years.'

'Have you tried to?'

She shook her head. 'I knew it was well and truly finished between us. I came to see he'd been on the rebound and—' her voice shook a little '—it was only a fling for him. I had no choice but to—' She broke off to smile bleakly. 'No choice but take it on the chin and retire. The only thing was—'

'You didn't know you were pregnant?' Cam Hillier said with some cynicism.

She ignored the cynicism. 'Oh, yes, I did.' She took a sip of brandy and prayed she wouldn't cry. She sniffed and patted her face to deflect any tears.

'You didn't tell him?' Cam queried with a frown.

'I did tell him. He said the only thing to do in the circumstances was have an abortion. He—he did offer to help me through it, but he also revealed that he was not only making a fresh start with this other woman, he was moving interstate and taking up a new position. He—I got the impression he even thought I may have tried to trap him into marriage. So...' She shrugged. 'I refused. I said, Don't worry! I can cope! And I walked out. That was the last time I saw him.'

Cam Hillier was silent.

'Although,' Liz said, 'I did go away for a month, and then I changed campuses and became an external student, so I have no idea if he tried to contact me again before he moved.'

'He still doesn't know you had the baby?'

'No.'

'Do you want to keep it from him for ever?'

'Yes!' Liz moved restlessly and stared down at her glass, then put it on the coffee table. 'When Scout was born all I could think was that she was *mine*. He'd never even wanted her to see the light of day, so why should he share her?' She gestured. 'I still feel that way, but...' She paused painfully. 'One day I'm going to have to think of it from Scout's point of view. When she's older and can understand things, she may want to know about her father.'

'But you don't want him to know in the meantime? That's why you took such astonishingly evasive measures tonight.' Cam Hillier rested his jaw on his fist. 'Do you think he'd react any differently?'

Liz heaved a sigh. 'I don't know, but it's hard to imagine anyone resisting Scout. She—she looks like him sometimes. And I did read an article about him fairly recently. He's beginning to make a name for himself in his chosen field. He and his wife have been married for four years. They have no children. There may be a dozen reasons for that, and I may be paranoid, but I can't help it—I'm scared stiff they'll somehow lure Scout away from me.'

'Liz.' He sat forward. 'You're her mother. They can't—unless you can't provide for her.'

'Maybe not legally, but there could be other ways. As she grows up she might find she prefers what they have to offer. They have a settled home. He has growing prestige. Whereas I am...I'm just getting by.' The raw, stark emotion was plain to see in her eyes.

'Have you got over him, Liz?'

A complete silence blanketed the room until the hoot from a harbour ferry broke it.

'I haven't forgotten or forgiven.' She stared out at the pool. 'Not that I was—not that I *wasn't* incredibly naïve and foolish. I haven't forgiven myself for that.'

'You should. These things happen. Not always with such consequences, but life has its lessons along the way.'

And, to her surprise, there was something like understanding in his eyes.

She moistened her lips and took several breaths to steady herself, because his lack of judgement of her was nearly her undoing. She gazed down at her bare feet and fought to control her tears.

Then she bit her lip as where she was, who *he* was, and how she'd poured all her troubles out to a virtual stranger with the added complication of him being her employer hit her.

Her eyes dilated and she took a ragged breath and straightened. 'I'm sorry,' she said huskily. 'If you want to sack me I'd understand, but do you believe me now?'

'Yes.' Cam Hillier didn't hesitate. 'Uh—no, I don't want to sack you. But I'll take you home now.' He drained the last of his brandy and stood up.

'Oh, I can get a taxi,' she assured him hastily, and followed suit.

He raised an eyebrow. 'With only one shoe? Your other one is ruined.'

'I—'

'Don't argue,' he recommended. He shrugged into his jacket, but didn't bother with his tie. Then he glanced at his watch. At the same time his mobile rang. He got it out of his pocket and looked at the screen.

'Ah, Portia,' he murmured. 'Wanting to berate me or make disparaging comparisons, do you think?' He clicked the phone off and shoved it into his pocket.

Liz took a guilty breath. 'I shouldn't have told you that. And—and she might want to explain. I think you should talk to her.'

He looked down at her, his deep blue eyes alight with mocking amusement. 'Your concern for my love-life is touching, Miss Montrose, but Portia and I have come to the end of the road. After you.' He gestured for her to precede him.

Liz clicked her tongue exasperatedly and tried to walk out as regally as was possible with no shoes on.

Cam Hillier dropped her off at her apartment building, and waited and watched as she crossed the pavement towards the entrance.

She'd insisted on putting on both shoes, although one still squelched a bit. He drummed his fingers on the steering wheel as it occurred to him that her long legs were just as good as Portia's. In fact, he thought, her figure might not be as voluptuous as Portia's but she was quite tall, with straight shoulders, a long, narrow waist. And the whole was slim and elegant—how had he not noticed it before?

Because he'd been put off by her glasses, her scraped-back hair, an unspoken but slightly militant air—or all three?

He grimaced, because he couldn't doubt now that under that composed, touch-me-not Ice Queen there existed real heartbreak. He'd seen that kind of heart-break before. The other thing he couldn't doubt was that she'd sparked his interest. Was it the challenge, though? Of breaking through the ice until he created a warm, loving woman? Was it because he sensed a response in her whether she liked it or not?

Whatever, he reflected, in a little over two weeks she was destined to walk out of his life. Unless…

He didn't articulate the thought as he finally drove off.

The next morning Liz placed a boiled egg with a face drawn on it in front of her daughter. Scout clapped her hands delightedly.

At the same time Mary Montrose said, 'You must have been late last night, Liz? I didn't even hear you come in.'

Yes, thank heavens, Liz thought. She'd been curiously unwilling to share the events of the evening with her mother—not to mention to expose the mess she'd been in, ripped, torn and with one soaked shoe.

Now, though, she gave Mary a much abridged version of the evening.

Mary sat up excitedly. 'I once designed an outfit for Narelle Hastings. Did you say she's Cameron Hillier's great-aunt?'

'So he said.' Liz smiled inwardly as she decapitated Scout's egg and spread the contents on toast soldiers. Her mother was an avid follower of the social scene.

'Let's see…' Mary meditated for a moment. 'I believe Narelle was his mother's aunt—that *would* make her his great-aunt. Well! There you go! Of course there've been a couple of tragedies for the Hastings/Hillier clan.'

Liz wiped some egg from Scout's little face and dropped a kiss on her nose. 'Good girl, you made short work of that! Like what?' she asked her mother.

'Cameron's parents were killed in an aircraft accident,

and his sister in an avalanche of all things. What's he like?'

Liz hesitated as she realised she wasn't at all sure what to make of Cameron Hillier. 'He's OK,' she said slowly, and looked at her watch. 'I'll have to make tracks shortly. So! What have you two girls got on today?'

'Koalas,' Scout said. She was as fair as Liz, with round blue eyes. Her hair was a cloud of curls and she glowed with health.

Liz pretended surprise. 'You're going to buy a koala?'

'No, Mummy,' Scout corrected lovingly. 'We're going to see them at the zoo! Aren't we, Nanna?'

'As well as all sorts of other animals, sweetheart,' her grandmother confirmed fondly. 'I'm looking forward to it myself!'

Liz took a breath as she thought of the sunny day outside, the ferry-ride across the harbour to Taronga Zoo, and how she'd love to be going with them. She bit her lip, then glanced gratefully at her mother. 'There are times when I don't know how to thank you,' she murmured.

'You don't have to,' Mary answered. 'You know that.'

Liz blinked, then got up to get ready for work.

The flat she and Scout shared with her mother was in an inner Sydney suburb. It was comfortable—her mother had seen to that—but the neighbourhood couldn't be described as classy...something Mary often lamented. But it was handy for the suburb of Paddington, for Oxford

Street and its trendy shopping and vibrant cafés. There were also markets, and history that included the Victoria Army Barracks and fine old terrace houses. If you were a sports fan, the iconic Sydney Cricket Ground was handy, as well as Centennial and Moore Parks. They often took picnics to the park.

The flat had three bedrooms and a small study. They'd converted the study into a bedroom for Scout, and the third bedroom into a workroom for Mary. It resembled an Aladdin's cave, Liz sometimes thought. There were racks of clothes in a mouth-watering selection of colours and fabrics. There was a rainbow selection of buttons, beads, sequins, the feathers Mary fashioned into fascinators, ribbons and motifs.

Mary had a small band of customers she 'created' for, as she preferred to put it. Gone were the heady days after Liz's father's death, when Mary had followed a life-long dream and invested in her own boutique. It hadn't prospered—not because the clothes weren't exquisite, but because, as her father had known, Mary had no business sense at all. Not only hadn't it prospered, it had all but destroyed Mary's resources.

But the two people Mary Montrose loved creating for above all were her daughter and granddaughter.

So it was that, although Liz operated on a fairly tight budget, no one would have guessed it from her clothes. And she went to work the day after the distressing scenario that had played out between two harbourside mansions looking the essence of chic, having decided it was a bit foolish to play down the originality of her clothes now.

She wore slim black pants to hide the graze on her knee, and a black and white blouson top with three-quarter sleeves, belted at the waist. Her shoes were black patent wedges with high cork soles—shoes she adored—and she wore a black and white, silver and bead Pandora-style bracelet.

As she finished dressing, she went to pin back her hair—then thought better of that too. There seemed to be no point now. She also put in her contact lenses.

But as she rode the bus to work she was thinking not of how she looked but other things. Cam Hillier in particular.

She'd tossed and turned quite a lot last night, as her overburdened mind had replayed the whole dismal event several times.

She had to acknowledge that he'd been... He hadn't been critical, had he? She couldn't deny she'd got herself into a mess—not only last night, of course, but in her life, and Scout's—which could easily invite criticism...

What did he really think? she wondered, and immediately wondered why it should concern her. After her disastrous liaison with Scout's father she'd not only been too preoccupied with her first priority—Scout, and building a life for both of them—but she'd had no interest in men. Once bitten twice shy, had been her motto. She'd even perfected a technique that had become, without her realising it until yesterday, she thought ironically, patently successful—Ice Queen armour.

It had all taken its toll, however, despite her joy in Scout. Not only in the battle to keep afloat economically, but also with her guilt at having to rely on her mother for help, therefore restricting her mother's life too. She had the feeling that she was growing old before her time, that she would never be able to let her hair down and enjoy herself in mixed company because of the cloud of bitterness that lay on her soul towards men.

So why was she now thinking about a man as she hadn't for years?

Why was she now suddenly physically vulnerable to a man she didn't really approve of, to make matters worse?

She paused her thoughts as a mental image of Cam Hillier came to her, and she had to acknowledge on a suddenly indrawn breath that he fascinated her in a curious sort of love/hate way—although of course it couldn't be love… But just when she wanted to hurl a brick at him for his sheer bloody-minded arrogance he did something, as he had last night, that changed a person's opinion of him. He hadn't been judgemental. He'd even made it possible for her spill her heart to him.

It was more too, she reflected. Not only his compelling looks and physique, but a vigorous mind that worked at the speed of lightning, an intellect you longed to have the freedom to match. Something about him that made you feel alive even if you were furious.

She gazed unseeingly out of the window and thought, what did it matter? She'd shortly be gone from his life. And even if she stayed within his orbit there was always the thorny question of Portia Pengelly—or if not Portia whoever her replacement would be.

She smiled a wintry little smile and shrugged, with not the slightest inkling of what awaited her shortly.

Ten minutes later she buzzed for a lift on the ground floor of the tower that contained the offices of the Hillier Corporation. One came almost immediately from the basement car park, and she stepped into it to find herself alone with her boss as the doors closed smoothly.

'Miss Montrose,' he said.

'Mr Hillier,' she responded.

He looked her up and down, taking in her stylish outfit, the sheen of her hair and her glossy mouth. And his lips quirked as he said, 'Hard to connect you with the wall-climbing cat burglar of last night.'

Liz directed him a tart little look before lowering her carefully darkened lashes, and said nothing.

'So I take it you're quite restored, Liz?'

'Yes,' she said coolly, and wasn't going to elaborate, but then thought better of it. 'Thank you. You were...' She couldn't think of the right word. 'Thank you.'

'That's all right.'

The lift slid to a stop and the doors opened, revealing the Hillier foyer, but for some strange reason neither of them made a move immediately. Not so strange, though, Liz thought suddenly. In the sense that it had happened to her before, in his car last evening, when she'd been trapped in a bubble of acute awareness of Cameron Hillier.

His suit was different today—slate-grey, worn with a pale blue shirt and a navy and silver tie—but it was just as beautifully tailored and moulded his broad shoulders just as effectively. There was a narrow black leather belt around his lean waist, and his black shoes shone and looked to be handmade.

But it wasn't a case of clothes making the man, Liz thought. It was the other way around. Add to that the tingling fresh aura of a man who'd showered and shaved recently, the comb lines in his thick hair, those intriguing blue eyes and his long-fingered hands... Her eyes widened as she realised even his hands impressed her. All of him stirred her senses in a way that made her long to have some physical contact with him—a touch, a mingling of their breath as they kissed...

Then their gazes lifted to each other's and she could see a nerve flickering in his jaw—a nerve that told her he was battling a similar compulsion. She'd known from the way he'd looked at her last night that he was no longer seeing her as a stick of furniture, but to think that he wanted her as she seemed to want him was electrifying.

It was as the lift doors started to close that they came out of their long moment of immobility. He pressed a button and the doors reversed their motion. He gestured for her to step out ahead of him.

She did so with a murmured thank-you, and headed for her small office. They both greeted Molly Swanson.

'Uh—give me ten minutes, then bring the diary in, Liz. And coffee, please, Molly.' He strode through into his office.

'How did it go? Last night?' Molly enquired. 'By the way, I've already had three calls from Miss Pengelly!'

'Oh, dear.' Liz grimaced. 'I'm afraid it might be over.'

'Probably just as well,' Molly said with a wise little look in her eyes. 'What he needs is a proper wife, not these film star types—I never thought she could act her way out of a paper bag, anyway!'

Liz blinked, but fortunately Molly was diverted by the discreet buzzing of her phone.

Eight minutes later, Liz gathered herself in readiness to present herself to her employer with the diary.

She'd poured herself a cup of cold water from the cooler, but instead of drinking it she'd dipped her hanky into it and splashed her wrists and patted her forehead.

I must be mad, she'd thought. *He* must be mad even to contemplate getting involved with me. Or is all he has in mind a replacement for Portia? Someone to deflect all the women he attracts—and I refuse to believe it's only because of his money.

Things were back to thoroughly businesslike as they went through his engagements for the day one by one, and he sipped strong black aromatic coffee from a Lalique glass in a silver holder.

'All right,' he said. 'Have you got the briefs for the Fortune conference?'

She nodded.

'I'll want you there. There's quite a bit of paper-work to be passed around and collected, et cetera. And I'll need you to drive me to and pick me up from the

Bromwich lunch. There's no damn parking to be found for miles.'

'Fine,' she murmured, then hesitated.

He looked up. 'A problem?'

'You want me to drive your car?'

'Why not?'

'To be honest—' Liz bit her lip '—I'd be petrified of putting a scratch on it.'

He sat back. 'Hadn't thought of that. So would I—to be honest.' He looked wry. 'Uh—get a car from the car pool.'

Liz relaxed. 'I think that's a much better idea.'

His lips twitched, and she thought he was going to say something humorous, but the moment passed and he looked at her in the completely deadpan way he had that had a built-in annoyance factor for anyone on the receiving end of it.

Liz was not immune to the annoyance as she found herself reduced to the status of a slightly troublesome employee. Then, if anything, she got more annoyed— but with herself. She had been distinctly frosty in the lift before they'd found themselves trapped in that curious moment of physical awareness, hadn't she?

She had told herself they would both be mad even to contemplate anything like a relationship—and she believed that. But some little part of her was obviously hankering to be treated... How? As a friend?

If I were out on a beach I'd believe I'd got a touch of the sun, she thought grimly. This man doesn't work that way, and there's no reason why he should.

She cleared her throat and said politely, 'What time would you like to leave?'

'Twelve-thirty.' He turned away.

The Fortune conference was scheduled for nine-thirty, and Liz and Molly worked together to prepare the conference room.

It got underway on time and went relatively smoothly. Liz did her bit, distributing and retrieving documents, providing water and coffee—and coping with the over-effusive thanks she got from the short, dumpy, middle-aged vice-President of the Fortune Seafood Group.

She only smiled coolly in return, but something—some prickling of her nervous system—caused her to look in Cam Hillier's direction, to find his gaze on her, steadfast and disapproving. Until a faint tide of colour rose in her cheeks, and he looked away at last.

Surely he couldn't think she was courting masculine approval or something stupid like that?

On the other hand, she reminded herself, she might find it stupid, but it could be an occupational hazard of being a single mother—men wondering if you were promiscuous...

It became further apparent that her boss was not in a good mood when she drove him to the Bromwich lunch in a company Mercedes. The reasons for this were two-fold.

'Hmm...' he said. 'You're a very cautious driver, Ms Montrose.'

Liz looked left and right and left again, and drove

across an intersection. 'It's not my car, your life is in my hands, Mr Hillier, and I have a certain respect for my own.'

'Undue caution can be its own hazard,' he commented. 'Roger is a better driver.'

Liz could feel her temper rising, but she held on to it. She said nothing.

He went on, 'Come to think of it, I don't have to worry about Roger receiving indecent proposals from visiting old-enough-to-know-better seafood purveyors either. Uh—you could have driven a bus through that gap, Liz.'

She lost it without any outward sign. She nosed the Mercedes carefully into the kerb, reversed it to a better angle, then switched off and handed him the keys.

She didn't shout, she didn't bang anything, but she did say, 'If you want to get to the Bromwich lunch in one piece, *you* drive. And don't ever ask me to drive you anywhere again. Furthermore, I can handle indecent proposals—any kind of proposals!—so you don't have a thing to worry about. As for the aspersions you cast on my driving, I happen to think *you're* a menace on the road.'

'Liz—'

But she ignored him as she opened her door and stepped out of the car.

CHAPTER THREE

TWO MINUTES LATER he was in the driver's seat, she was in the passenger seat, and she had no idea if he was fighting mad or laughing at her—although she suspected the latter.

'Right,' he said as he eased the car back into the traffic. 'Get onto Bromwich and tell them I'm not coming.'

Liz gasped. 'Why not? You can't—'

'I can. I never did want to go to their damn lunch anyway.'

'But you agreed!' she reminded him.

'All the same, they'll be fine without me. It is a lunch for two hundred people. I could quite easily have got lost in the crowd,' he said broodingly.

Liz thought, with irony, that it was highly unlikely, but she said tautly, 'And what will I tell them?'

'Tell them...' he paused, 'I've had a row with my diary secretary, during which she not only threatened to take me apart but I got told I was a *menace*, and that I'm feeling somewhat diminished and unable to contemplate socialising on a large scale as a result.'

Liz looked at him with extreme frustration. 'Apart

from anything else, that has *got* to be so untrue!' she said through her teeth.

He grimaced. 'You could also tell them,' he added, 'that since it's a nice day I've decided the beach is a better place for lunch. We'll go and have some fish and chips. Like fish and chips?'

She lifted her hands in a gesture of despair. 'I suppose nothing will persuade you this is a very bad idea?'

'Nothing,' he agreed, then grinned that lightning crooked grin. 'Maybe you should have thought of that before you had a hissy fit and handed over the car.'

'You were being enough to—you were impossible!'

'Mmm…' He said it meditatively, and with a faint frown. 'I seem to be slightly off-key today. Do you have the same problem? After what happened in the lift?' he added softly.

Liz studied the road ahead, and wondered what would happen if she admitted to him that she had no idea how to cope with the attraction that had sprung up between them. Yes, it might have happened to her for the first time in a long time, but did that mean she wasn't scared stiff of it? Of course she was. She knew it. She clenched her hands briefly in her lap. Besides, what could come of it?

An affair at the most, she reasoned. Cameron Hillier was not going to marry a single mother who sometimes struggled to pay her bills. Marry! Dear heaven, what was she thinking? Even with the best intentions and no impediments they had to be a long way from *that*.

And, having thought of her bills, she couldn't stop

herself from thinking of them again—that and the fact that she had no other job lined up yet.

Just get yourself out of this without losing your job if you can, Liz, she recommended to herself.

'I apologise for losing my temper,' she said at last. 'I—I'm probably not a very good driver. I haven't had a lot of experience, but I was doing my best.' She looked ruefully heavenwards.

Cam Hillier cast her a swift glance that was laced with mockery. 'That's all?'

She swallowed, fully understanding the mockery—she was dodging the issue of what had happened between them in the lift and he knew it.

She twisted her hands together, but said quite evenly, 'I'm afraid so.'

There was silence in the car until he said, 'That has a ring of finality to it. In other words we're never destined to be more than we are, Ms Montrose?'

Liz pushed her hair behind her ears. 'We're not,' she agreed barely audibly. 'Oh.' She reached for her purse—anything to break the tension of the moment. 'I'll ring Bromwich—although I may not get anyone at this late stage.'

'So be it,' he said, and she knew he wasn't talking about the lunch he was going to miss.

She hesitated, but decided she might as well cement her stance on the matter—in a manner of speaking... 'You don't have to take me to lunch, Mr Hillier. I'd quite understand.'

'Not at all, Ms Montrose,' he drawled. 'For one thing, I'm starving. And, since Roger and I often have lunch when we're on the road together, you don't need to view it with any suspicion.'

'Suspicion?'

This time he looked at her with satirical amusement glinting in his blue eyes. 'Suspicion that I might try to chat you up or—break down your icy ramparts.'

Liz knew—she could feel what was happening to her—and this time nothing in the world could have stopped her from blushing brightly. She took refuge from the embarrassment of it by contacting the Bromwich lunch venue.

The restaurant he took her to had an open area on a boardwalk above the beach. They found a table shaded by a canvas umbrella, ordered, and looked out over the sparkling waters of Sydney Harbour. They could see the Opera House and the Harbour Bridge.

And he was as good as his word. He didn't try to chat her up or break her down, but somehow made it possible for them to be companionable as they ate their fish and chips.

He was so different, Liz thought, from how he could be at other times. Not only had he left the arrogant multi-millionaire of the office behind, but also the moody persona he'd been in the car. He even looked younger, and she found herself catching her breath once or twice—once when an errant breeze lifted his dark hair, and once when he played absently with the salt cellar in his long fingers.

'Well…' He consulted his watch finally. 'Let's get back to work.'

'Thanks for that.' She stood up.

He followed suit, and for one brief moment they looked into each other's eyes—a searching, perfectly sober exchange—before they both looked away again, and started to walk to the car.

Liz knew she was to suffer the consequences of that pleasant lunch in the form of a yet another restless night.

Not so Scout, though. She was still bubbling with excitement at what she'd seen at the zoo, and she fell asleep almost as soon as her head touched the pillow.

Liz dropped a kiss on her curls and tiptoed out. But when she went to bed she tossed and turned for ages as flashes of what had been an extraordinary day came back to haunt her.

Such as when that light breeze had ruffled his hair and it had affected her so curiously—given her goose-bumps, to be precise. Such as when he'd played absently with the salt cellar and she'd suffered a mental flash of having his hands on her naked body.

I've got to deal with this, she told herself, going hot and cold again. I don't think I can get out of this job without affecting my rating with the agency, and without having to take less money—which would play havoc with my budget. I've got to think of Scout and what's best for her. A brief affair with a man who, if you go on his present track record, doesn't appear to be able to commit? Not to Portia Pengelly, anyway, and that means he was using her—he more or less admitted that.

I've got to remember what it felt like to find out

I'd been used, and to be told an abortion was the only course of action in the circumstances...

She stared into the darkness, then closed her eyes on the tears that came.

She resumed her monologue when her tears subsided. So, Liz, even if you are no longer the Ice Queen you were, you've got to get through this. Don't let another man bring you down.

She was helped by the fact that Cam Hillier was away for the next couple of days, but when he came back she still had two weeks left to work for him.

He seemed to be in a different mood, though. Less abrasive—with her, anyway—and there were no *double entendres*, no signs that they'd ever stood in a lift absolutely mesmerised by each other.

Had he made it up with Portia? she wondered. Did that account for his better mood? Or had he found a replacement for Portia?

Whatever it was, Liz relaxed a bit, and she did not take exception when they got caught in a traffic jam on the way to a meeting, and to kill the time he asked her about her earlier life.

It was a dull day and had rained overnight. There was an accident up ahead and the traffic was hopelessly gridlocked. There was a helicopter flying overhead.

'It must be a serious accident,' Liz murmured. 'We could be late.'

He switched off the motor and shrugged. 'Nothing we can do,' he said, with uncharacteristic patience. 'Tell me how you grew up?'

Liz pleated the skirt of the red dress she wore with a light black jacket, and thought, Why not?

'Uh…let's see,' she said reflectively. 'My father was a teacher and very academic, whilst my mother…' She paused, because sometimes it was hard to sum up her mother. 'She's this intensely creative person—*so* good with her hands but not terribly practical.'

She smiled. 'You wouldn't have thought it could work between them, but it did. She could always liven him up, and he could always deflect her from her madder schemes. As a teacher, of course, he was really keen on education, and he coached me a lot. That's how I came to go to a private school on a scholarship. I also went to uni on scholarships. He—' She stopped.

'Go on,' Cam murmured after a few moments.

She cast him an oblique little glance, wondering at the same time why he was interested in this—why she was even humouring him…

'I used to think I took more after him—we read together and studied things together—but lately some of Mum has started to shine through. She's an inspired cook, and I'm interested in it now—although I'll never be the seamstress she is.'

'So how did you cope with getting your degree and being a single mum?' he queried. 'Simple arithmetic suggests Scout must have intervened somewhere along the line.'

Liz looked at his hands on the steering wheel and switched her gaze away immediately. Was this just plain curiosity, or…? But was there any reason not to give him the bare bones of it anyway?

'It was hard work, but in some ways it kept me sane. It was a goal I could still achieve, I guess—although I had to work part-time.' She paused and looked rueful. 'At all sorts of crazy jobs at the same time.'

'Such as?'

'I was a receptionist in a tattoo parlour once.' She looked nostalgic for a moment. 'I actually got a bunch of flowers from a group of bikies I came to know there when Scout was born. Uh—I worked in a bottle shop, a supermarket. I did some nanny work, house cleaning.'

She stopped and gestured. 'My father had died by then—he never knew Scout—but I was determined to get my degree because I knew how disappointed he would have been if I hadn't.'

'How did you get into this kind of work?'

Liz smiled. 'I had a lucky break. One of my lecturers had contacts with the agency, and a good idea of the kind of replacement staff they supplied. She schooled me on most aspects of a diary secretary's duties, my mother set me up with a suitable wardrobe, and *voilà*!—as they say.'

'Helped along by being as bright as a tack.' He said it almost to himself. 'I gather you take time off between assignments?'

She nodded. 'I always try for a couple of weeks—not only to give my mother a break, but to be able to spend more time with Scout myself.'

'So she still makes your clothes? Your mother?'

'Yes. She made that jacket.' Liz explained how she'd come to have it with her on the day of the cocktail party. 'She actually made it for the part-time weekend job I have as cashier at a very upmarket restaurant.'

'Your father would be proud of you.'

'I don't know about that.'

'And Scout's father? Any more sightings?'

Liz shook her head but looked uneasy. 'I'm wondering if he's moved back to Sydney and that's why he was at your great-aunt's party.'

'I can find out, if you like. But even if he has Sydney's a big city.' He flicked her an interrogative look.

'No. No, thanks. I think I'll just let sleeping dogs lie. Oh, look—they're diverting the traffic. We could be just in time.'

He seemed about to say something, then he shrugged and switched on the motor.

As often happened when something came up out of the blue, things came in pairs, Liz discovered that same evening. She heard a radio interview with Scout's father in which he talked mainly about the economy—he was an economist—but also about his move back to his hometown from Perth. And the fact that he had no children as yet, but he and his wife were still hoping for some.

She'd flicked the radio off and tried to concentrate on the fact that her only emotion towards Scout's father was now distaste—tried to concentrate on it in order to disguise the cold little bubble of fear the rest of it had brought her.

The next morning her boss made an unusual request.

She was tidying away the clutter on his desk, prior to a meeting with his chief of Human Resources, when he took a phone call that didn't seem to be business-orientated.

'Broke the window?' he said down the line, with a surprised lift of his eyebrows. 'I wouldn't have thought he was strong enough to— Well, never mind. Tell him not to try it again until I'm there.' He put down the phone and watched Liz abstractedly for a few minutes, and then with a frown of concentration.

Liz, becoming aware of this, looked down at her exemplary outfit—a summer suit. Matching jacket and A-line skirt. There didn't seem to be anything wrong with it—no buttons undone, no bra strap showing or anything like that. So she looked back at him with a query in her eyes.

He drummed his fingers on the desk. 'Do you remember a song about a boomerang that wouldn't come back?'

She blinked and thought for a moment, then shook her head. 'No.'

'I seem to,' he said slowly. 'See if you can find it, please.'

Liz opened her mouth, but she was forestalled by the arrival of his chief of Human Resources.

Later that day she was able to tell him she'd found the boomerang song, and was rather charmed by it. 'It's a golden oldie. Charlie Drake was the artist,' she said. 'Not only wouldn't his boomerang come back, but he hit the Flying Doctor.'

'Excellent,' Cam Hillier said. But that was all he said, leaving Liz completely mystified.

* * *

Some days later he surprised her again.

She was a bit preoccupied, because just before she'd left for work and had been checking her purse she'd found she'd inadvertently picked up a note meant for her mother. It was from an old friend of her mother's who ran a dancing school, and it concerned the school's annual concert. Would Mary be interested in designing the costumes for the concert? It would mean about three months' work, it said.

But Mary Montrose had penned a reply on the back of it.

So sorry. Would have loved to but I just don't have the time these days. All good wishes...

She hadn't posted it yet.

Only because of looking after Scout could she not do it, Liz thought to herself, and flinched. But what to do? Scout spent two mornings a week at a daycare centre; more Liz could not afford. And those two free mornings a week would not be enough to allow Mary to take on a job she would have loved.

Liz had replaced the note on the hall table, feeling jolted and miserable, and came to work.

It was after she'd gone through the day's schedule with her boss that he asked to see the next day's schedule.

Liz handed the diary over.

He scanned it in silence for a minute or two, then said decisively, 'Reschedule the lot.' He handed the book back to her.

Liz actually felt herself go pale. 'The lot?'

'That's what I said.' He sat back in his chair.

'But...' Liz stopped and bit her lip. There were at least ten appointments in one form or another to be re-scheduled. There were at least five major appointments amongst them, involving third, fourth and even fifth parties, so cancellation would produce a ripple effect of chaos down the line.

She swallowed. 'All right. Uh—what will you being doing tomorrow? I mean, what would you like me to say? Mr Hillier has been called away urgently? Or...' She paused and gazed at him.

That crooked grin chased across Cam Hillier's lips, but he said gravely, 'Yep. Especially said in those cool, well-bred tones. It should do the trick admirably.'

Liz frowned. 'I don't sound—are you saying I sound snooty?'

'Yes, you do.' He raised an eyebrow at her. 'Probably your private school.'

She grimaced, and after a moment deliberately changed the subject. 'Should I know what you *are* doing tomorrow, Mr Hillier, or would you rather I remained in ignorance?'

He noted the change of subject with a twist of his lips. 'That would be hard, because you'll be with me. I'm going up to Yewarra and I need your help, I'll be engaging staff.'

'Yewarra?' she repeated, somewhat dazedly.

'It's an estate I have in the Blue Mountains.'

'The Blue...' Liz caught herself sounding like a parrot and changed tack. 'I mean—how long will it take?'

'Just a day—just working hours,' he replied smoothly, and shrugged. 'Let's leave here at eight a.m.—then we *will* be back in working hours. And come casual.'

'You're planning to drive up there?' she queried.

'Uh-huh. Why not?'

Liz moved uneasily. 'I prefer not to feel as if I'm low-flying when I'm in a car.'

He grinned. 'I promise to obey the speed limits tomorrow. Anyway, it's a very good car and I'm a very good driver.'

Liz opened her mouth to say his modesty was amazing but she changed her mind. As she knew to her cost, you could never quite tell how Cam Hillier was going to react in a confrontation...

'So,' he said, lying back in his chair with his hands behind his head, 'only three more days before Roger is restored to our midst—completely recovered from his glandular fever, so he assures me.'

'Yes,' she said quietly.

'And you head off into the sunset, Liz.'

'That too,' she agreed.

'But we've worked well together. Oh—' he sat up and gestured widely '—apart from the couple of times you've narrowly restrained yourself from slapping my face, and the day you threatened me with worse.' His blue eyes were alive with satanic amusement.

'I get the feeling you're never going to let me forget that, so it's just as well I *am* riding off into the sunset or something like that.'

She was destined not to know what his response

would have been, because the door of his office burst open and Portia Pengelly swept in.

'Cam, I have to speak to you—*oh*!' Portia stopped dead, then advanced slowly and ominously with that knee-in-front-of-knee model's walk. She wore a simple black silk shift dress splashed with vibrant colours. She had a bright watermelon cardigan draped over her shoulders, and carried a large tote in the same colour. Her famous straw-coloured locks were gorgeously dishevelled and her long legs were bare.

'Who is *this*?' she demanded as she gazed at Liz.

Liz got up and took up the diary. 'I work here. Uh—if that'll be all, Mr Hillier, I'll get back to work. Excuse me,' she said to Portia, and left the room—but not quite quickly enough to miss Portia Pengelly uttering Cam Hillier's Christian name in what sounded like an impassioned plea.

They set off on the dot of eight the next morning.

Liz had taken her boss's advice to 'come casual' to heart. She wore a short-sleeved pale grey jumper with a black and white bow pattern on the front, and slimline jeans with a broad cuff that came, fashionably, to just above her ankles. She had a cardigan to match the jumper, a black leather bag, and pale grey leather flatties.

He also wore jeans, with a denim shirt, and he slung a leather jacket into the back of the Aston Martin.

They didn't say much as he negotiated the traffic out of Sydney—with decorum, she noted, and relaxed somewhat—and headed west. Once they were beyond Penrith the road started to climb—and the Blue Mountains started to live up to their name.

Liz had read somewhere that their distinctive blue haze was the result of the release of oils into the air from the forests of eucalypts that cloaked their slopes. She'd further read, though, that they were not so much mountains but the rugged ramparts, scored and slashed with gullies and ravines, of a vast plateau.

Whatever, she thought, as the powerful vehicle chewed up the kilometres effortlessly and the road got steeper, they were awe-inspiring and yet somehow secretive at the same time, cloaked in their blue haze. And indeed they had proved to be. Until 1994 they'd kept in their remote and isolated valleys the secret of the Wollemi pine—a living fossil said to date back to Gondwana and the time of the dinosaur.

It was when they'd almost reached their destination that he said out of the blue, 'What's your next assignment, Liz?'

She grimaced. 'I don't have one yet. But I'm sure something will come up,' she added. 'It's just hard to predict at times.'

'How will you manage if something doesn't come up for some time?'

Liz moved restlessly. 'I'll be fine.' She paused, then cast him a cool little look. 'Please, I do appreciate your concern, but I think it's best left alone. I'll be gone in a couple of days and it's difficult for me—for both of us, probably—to remain professional if this keeps cropping up between us.'

'Professional?' He drove for a mile or so. 'That flew

out of the window, in a manner of speaking, before any of *this* "cropped up".'

Liz frowned. 'What do you mean?'

He took his eyes off the road to look at her just long enough for her to see the irony in his eyes. 'Narelle was right. We're not cut out to be only employer and employee. There is, Ms Montrose, not to put too fine a point on it, a kind of electricity between us that started to sizzle right here in this car outside my house almost two weeks ago. Or perhaps even earlier—that day in the office when you put on your magic coat and let down your hair.'

CHAPTER FOUR

LIZ'S MOUTH fell open.

'And it continued the next morning in the lift,' he added, as he changed gear and they swept round a corner. 'In fact it's never gone away—despite your best efforts to kill it stone-dead.'

It struck Liz that they had driven through the pretty village of Leura with her barely noticing it, and were now on a country road. It also struck her that it was impossible to refute his claim.

She stared down at her hands. 'Look,' she said, barely audibly, 'you'd be mad to want to get involved with me. And vice versa.'

Out of the corner of her eye she saw that crooked grin come and go before he said, 'It doesn't work that way.'

'If we're two sane adults, it should,' she replied coolly. 'You can make choices, can't you?'

He changed gear again and slowed down. 'On the virtually nothing we have to go on? It'd be like a stab in the dark.' He turned the wheel and they coasted into a driveway barred by a pair of tall wrought-iron gates.

'Is this it?' Liz asked.

'This is it.' He pressed a buzzer mounted on the dashboard and the gates started to open. 'Welcome to Yewarra, Liz.'

For a moment Liz felt like escaping—escaping his car, his estate and Cam Hillier himself. She fleetingly felt overburdened, and as if she were entering a zone she had no control over.

Moments later, however, she was enchanted as he drove slowly up the gravelled driveway.

Beneath majestic trees there were beds of white and blue agapanthus. There was flowering jasmine and honeysuckle climbing up jacarandas bursting into pale violet bloom. There were gardenias and roses. It was a glorious riot of colour and perfume.

She turned to him, her face alight with appreciation. 'This is just—beautiful.'

He grimaced. 'Thanks. In a way it's a tribute to my mother. A tribute to her love of gardens and her innate sense of refined living that somehow survived the often harsh life she shared with my father.'

He pulled up beside a fountain. The house beyond it was two-storeyed and built of warm, earthy stone with a shingle roof. The windows were framed in timber and had wrought-iron security grids. The front door—a double door—was beautifully carved with a dolphin motif and had curved brass handles.

'The house isn't bad either,' she commented with a wry little smile. 'Did you build it?'

'No. And I've hardly done anything to it. Well, I changed that,' he amended, and gestured to the fountain.

'It was this rather nauseating circle of coy naked ladies clutching plump cherubs.'

What stood there now couldn't have been more different. A bronze dolphin leapt out of the water, cascading sparkling droplets.

Liz stared at it. 'Do dolphins have any special significance?'

He considered. 'It's not inappropriate for someone whose roots go back to a seafaring life, I guess.'

Liz thought of the paintings in his office in Sydney. 'But you've come a long way since then,' she offered quietly.

'A long way,' he agreed. But, although he said it easily enough, she thought she detected the faintest echo of a grim undertone.

At that moment the front doors flew open and a small boy of about five stood on the doorstep, waving excitedly at the same time as he was restrained by a nanny.

Liz's eyes widened. 'Who...?' she began, and bit her lip, not wanting to sound nosy.

'That's Archie,' Cam Hillier said. 'He's my sister's orphaned son. I've adopted him.'

He opened his door and got out, and Archie escaped his nanny's restraining hand and flew over the gravel, calling, 'Cam! Cam—am I glad to see you! Wenonah has had *six* puppies but they only want to let me keep one!'

Cam Hillier picked his nephew up and hugged him. 'But just think,' he said, 'of the five other kids who'd love to have a puppy but couldn't if you kept them all.'

Liz blinked. She'd assumed his nephew Archie would

be older. She certainly hadn't expected to see Cameron Hillier so at home with a five-year-old...

'I suppose that's true,' Archie said slowly. 'Oh, well, maybe I won't mind.' He hugged Cam. 'Are you staying?'

'Not tonight,' Cam said, but added as Archie's face fell, 'I'll be up for the weekend.' He put the little boy down. 'Archie, meet Liz—she works for me.'

'How do you do, Liz?' Archie said with impeccable manners. 'Would you like to see my menagerie?'

Both Cam and the nanny, still standing on the doorstep, opened their mouths to intervene, but Liz got in first. 'How do you do, Archie? I would indeed.'

Archie slid his hand into hers. 'It's down this path. I'll show you.'

'Not too long, Archie,' Cam said. 'Liz and I have work to do.'

Archie's menagerie was in a fenced-off compound not far from the house. There was netting stretched over the top, and there were shrubs growing within and without to shade it. Old hollow tree trunks lay inside. The paths were gravel. He had rabbits in hutches, and a family of guinea pigs in a marvellous cage fashioned like a castle, with climbing wheels and slides and bells. He had a white cockatoo with a sulphur crest and a limited vocabulary— 'Hello, cocky!' and 'Oh, golly gosh!' He had a pond with a small waterfall and slippery stones, with greenery growing through it all and six frogs enjoying it. In another pond he had goldfish.

'Did you do all this?' Liz asked, rather enchanted,

surveying the menagerie and thinking how much Scout would love it.

'No, silly. I'm only five,' Archie replied. 'Cam did most if it. But I helped. Here.' He handed Liz a guinea pig. 'That's Golly, and this one—' he drew another one out of the castle-like cage '—is Ginny. She's his wife and they're all the kids.' Archie pointed into the cage.

'I see,' Liz replied gravely as she stroked Golly. 'So where is Wenonah? And her puppies?'

'Down at the stables. Wenonah can be a bit naughty about rabbits and things. She likes to chase them. But I'm going to train the puppy I get not to. Thing is—' his brow creased '—I don't know whether to get a boy or a girl.'

'Perhaps Cam can help you there? He might have an idea on the subject.'

Archie brightened. 'He usually does. Now, this is something special—my blue-tongue lizard!'

'Oh, wow!' Liz carefully put Golly back and sank down on her knees. 'Oh, my!'

That was how Cam found them some time later, both Liz and Archie on their knees and laughing together as they tried to entice Wally the blue-tongue lizard out of his cave.

Liz looked up and got up, brushing her knees. 'Sorry, but this is fascinating. I was just thinking how much Scout would enjoy it.'

'Who's Scout?' Archie enquired. 'Does he like animals?'

'*She*—she's my little girl, and she adores animals at the moment.'

'You should bring her over to play with me,' Archie said.

'Oh—'

Cam intervened. 'We'll see, Archie. Can I have Liz now?'

Archie agreed, but grudgingly.

'You made a hit there,' Cam commented as they walked back to the house.

'You get into "little kid mode" if you're around them long enough,' Liz said humorously, and stepped through the dolphin doors—only to stop with a gasp.

The entrance hall was a gallery that led to a lounge below. It had a vast stone fireplace and some priceless-looking rugs scattered about the stone-flagged floor. It was furnished with sumptuously comfortable settees and just a few equally priceless-looking ornaments and paintings. The overall colour scheme was warm and inviting—cream and terracotta with dashes of mint-green. But it was the wall of ceiling-high windows overlooking the most stunning view that had made Liz gasp.

A valley dropped precipitously below that wall of windows and fled away into the morning sunlight in all its wild splendour.

'It's—amazing. Do you ever get used to it?' she asked.

'Not really. It changes—different lights, different times of day, different weather. Uh—the study is down those stairs.'

The study came as another surprise to Liz. It presented

quite a different view—a sunlit, peaceful view—across a formal garden to grassy paddocks with wooden fences and horses grazing, lazily switching their tails. Beyond the paddocks she could see a shingle-roofed building with two wings and a clock tower in the middle—obviously the stables.

She turned back from the windows and surveyed the study. It was wood-panelled and lined with books on two sides. On the other walls there were very similar paintings to those in his office in Sydney: horses and trawlers. Her lips twitched.

The carpet was Ming blue, and the chairs on either side of the desk were covered in navy leather.

She sat down as directed, and he took his place behind the desk.

'I don't know how you manage to tear yourself away from the place,' she commented, as he poured coffee from a pewter flask. She cocked her head to one side as she accepted her cup. 'Was the menagerie your idea?'

'More or less.' He stirred his coffee. 'Archie's always been interested in animals, so I thought instead of mice in shoeboxes we might as well do it properly.' He looked down at his mug, 'It has also, I think, helped him get over the loss of his mother.'

Liz hesitated, then decided not to pursue that. 'Well, I *am* here to work, so—' She broke off when she noticed an ironic little glint in his eye as he crossed his arms and simply watched her.

And it all came flooding back—what had been said in the car before her enchantment with his gardens and his nephew's menagerie had claimed her.

She closed her eyes as she felt the colour that flooded her cheeks. As her lashes fluttered up, she said with effort, 'Let's not go there, Mr Hillier. In fact I refuse to discuss it.'

He lay back in his chair, dangling a silver pen in his long fingers. 'Why? It *did* happen.'

'It was an aberration,' Liz said coolly, reverting to her Ice Queen role.

He grinned—a full version of that crooked but utterly charismatic smile this time. 'Just a bit of naughtiness between two people for reasons unknown?'

'Well,' Liz said, thinking fast, 'you *had* been stood up out of the blue. Could that have been at the back of your mind?'

'Portia couldn't have been further from my mind.' He drummed his fingers on the desk and shrugged. 'That may sound—'

'It sounds pretty cold-blooded,' she broke in.

He looked at her. 'Portia thought that in exchange for her—charms—she could persuade me to back a clothing range. Swimsuits, in fact. She had her heart set on designing and no doubt modelling them,' he said dryly. 'When I looked into it I found it was an overcrowded market and a poor investment. Despite the fact that I'd never made any promises of any kind, she took the view that I had—uh—two-timed her.'

Liz blinked. 'Oh?'

He raised an eyebrow at her. 'You sound surprised.'

'I am,' Liz confessed.

'You assumed it was all over another woman?'

he suggested, with a glint of wicked amusement in his eyes.

Liz bit her lip and looked annoyed, because she knew she was being mocked. All the same it *was* what she'd automatically assumed. 'Well...yes. But did you honestly expect her still to want to go out with you?' she added. 'I would have thought not.'

Cam Hillier dragged his hand through his hair with a rueful look. 'Yep—got that bit wrong,' he confessed. 'I thought she'd at least trust my judgement.' He shrugged. 'Where money's concerned anyway.'

'I see,' Liz said—quite inadequately, she felt. But what else could she say?

He sat back with a faint smile. 'And it is over between us.'

'But only yesterday it didn't sound as if it was over for her!' Liz protested.

'Look, it is now,' he said dryly. 'Believe me.'

Liz shivered suddenly as she watched his mouth set, and knew she couldn't disbelieve him.

'But don't for one minute imagine that Portia won't find someone else.' He paused and looked at her penetratingly. 'Probably a lot sooner than I will, since you're so hell-bent on being the Ice Queen.'

Liz's lips parted in sheer shock. 'How did you...?'

He shrugged. 'We've known each other for nearly a month now. Quite long enough for me to detect when you're in chilly mode.'

Liz blinked helplessly several times and opened her mouth—but he spoke first. 'Never mind, we'll leave all that aside. How are you with horses?'

She opened her mouth again—to repeat bewilderedly *Horses?*—but just stopped herself in time. 'I have no idea why you want to know,' she said, 'but I like horses. I rode as a kid. If, though, you're going to ask me about trawlers, I've never been on one and have no desire to do so!'

His eyebrows shot up. 'Why would I?'

Liz gestured to the walls. 'They seem to go together for you. Horses and trawlers. And, probably because I don't understand any of this, in a fog of bewilderment I thought they might come next.'

He looked quizzical. 'No, but I suppose they *do* go together for me. I inherited a trawler fleet from my father, which eventually made the horses possible.'

Liz gazed at him. 'Why Shakespeare, though?'

He looked surprised. 'You noticed?'

She nodded.

'My mother again,' he said. 'She was hot on Shakespeare.'

'I see.' Liz was silent for a moment, then, 'Do you want to tell me why it matters whether I like horses? Come to that, why you've pretty thoroughly gone through my background with a toothcomb—and why I have the feeling I'm up here under false pretences?' she added, as she was gripped by the sensation that all was not what it seemed.

'Well, it *is* about engaging staff, Liz. I'd like to offer you the position of managing this place.'

This time Liz was struck seriously speechless.

'It's not a domestic position, it's a logistic one,' he went on. 'I do quite a lot of entertaining up here, and we often have house parties. I have good household staff, but I need someone to co-ordinate things both here and in the stables.'

'How…how so?' she asked, her voice breaking and husky with surprise. 'I'm not that good with horses.'

'It's not to do with the horses *per se*. We stand three stallions, we have twenty of our own mares, and we agist outside mares in foal and with foals at foot. The paperwork to keep track of it all alone is a big job. Checking the pedigrees of prospective mares for our stallions—it goes on. I need someone who can organise all that on a computer program.'

Liz breathed deeply but said nothing.

'I need to free up my stud master and the people who actually work with the horses from the paperwork—and incidentally free them up from all the people who stream in and out of the place.'

'Ah.' It was all Liz could think of to say.

He cast her an ironic little look, but continued. 'There's a comfortable staff cottage that would go with the position—big enough for you and Scout, as well as your mother. There's even a ready-made friend for Scout in Archie,' he said, and gazed at her steadily.

'But—' She stopped to clear her throat. 'Why me?'

'You've impressed me,' he said, and shrugged. 'You're as good as Roger—if not better in some areas. I think you're wasted as a diary secretary. I think you have the organisational skills as well as the people skills to do the job justice.'

'I…' Liz pressed her hands together and took another

deep breath. 'I don't know what to say,' she confessed. 'It's the last thing I was expecting.'

'Let's talk remuneration, then.' And for the next few minutes he outlined a package that was generous. So much so that to knock it back would be not so much looking a gift horse in the mouth but kicking it in the teeth...

'We'd have a three-month trial period,' he said, and grinned. 'Just in case you hanker for the bright lights or whatever.'

'If I didn't bring my mother—' Liz heard herself say cautiously, then couldn't go on.

He eyed her narrowly. 'Why wouldn't you?'

She gestured, then told him about the note she'd intercepted. 'She's been so wonderful, but I know it's something she'd love to do—I just haven't been able to work out how.' She shook her head. 'It wouldn't work up here, either.'

'You could share Archie's nanny for the times when you couldn't be with Scout.'

Liz stared at him, her eyes suddenly dark and uncertain. 'Why are you doing this—really? Are there any strings attached?'

'Such as?' He said it barely audibly.

'Such as going down a slippery slope into your bed?'

They stared at each other and she saw his eyes harden, but he answered in a drawl, 'My dear Liz, if you imagine I'd need to go to all these lengths to do that, you're wrong.'

'What's that supposed to mean?'

'You know as well as I do that if we gave each other just the smallest leeway we wouldn't be able to help ourselves. *But*—and I emphasise this—' his voice hardened this time '—if you prefer to go on your solitary way, so be it.'

'You were the one who brought it up,' Liz said hotly, then looked uncomfortable.

'At least I'm honest,' he countered.

'I haven't been dishonest.'

'Not precisely,' he agreed, and simply waited for her reply.

Liz ground her teeth. 'What you may not know is that being a single mother lays you open to...to certain men thinking you're...promiscuous.'

She wasn't expecting any more surprises at this point, but she got one when Cameron Hillier leant forward suddenly, his blue eyes intent. 'I know quite a bit about single mothers. My sister was one—and that, I guess, even while I'm not prepared to be dishonest, is why I have some sympathy for you, Liz Montrose.'

Her mouth fell open. She snapped it shut. So that explained the understanding she thought she'd seen in his eyes when she'd told him her story!

'And, further towards complete honesty,' he went on, 'I need the right influence in Archie's life at the moment—which I think you could be. I can't be with him nearly as much as I should. He starts school next year, so that will distance us even more. I want this last year of his before school to be memorable for him. And safe. And happy.'

'You don't know—how do you know I could do that?'

He sat back. 'I saw you with him just now. I've seen, from the moment you first mentioned her, how much your daughter means to you. How it lights you up just to say her name.'

'I still…' She paused helplessly. 'It's come up so fast!'

'It's part of my success—the ability to sum things up and make quick decisions.'

Liz looked at him askance. 'Your modesty is amazing at times.'

'I know,' he agreed seriously, but she could suddenly see the glimmer of laughter in his eyes.

'Well—'

'Er…excuse me?' a strange voice said, and they both swung round to see a woman standing in the doorway. 'Lunch is ready, Mr Hillier. I've served it in the kitchen if that's all right with you?'

Cam Hillier rose. 'That's fine, Mrs Preston. Thank you.'

It was a huge kitchen—brick-walled, with a tiled floor and rich woodwork. Herbs grew in pots along the windowsills, a vast antique dresser displayed a lovely array of china, but all the appliances were modern and stainless steel.

There was a long refectory table at one end that seated six in ladder-back chairs with raffia seats.

The lady who answered to 'Mrs Preston', grey-haired, pink-cheeked and of comfortable girth, was dishing up steaks, Liz saw, and baked Idaho potatoes topped with sour cream and chives. A bowl brimming with salad—cos lettuce, tomatoes, cucumber, capsicum and shallots—was also set out, and there was a bread basket laden with fresh warm rolls.

The steaks, she realised from their tantalising aroma, had been marinated and grilled along with button mushrooms.

A bottle of red wine was breathing in a pottery container.

'Hungry?' Cam asked as they sat down.

'I've suddenly realised I'm starving,' she confessed and looked around. 'Where's Archie?'

'At the dentist in Leura—just for a check-up. Mrs Preston,' Cam added, 'may I tell Miss Montrose what you told me on the phone a couple of days ago?'

Mrs Preston blinked at Liz, then said, 'Of course.'

Cam reached for the bottle of wine and poured them each a glass. 'For quite some years now Mrs Preston has been housekeeper and most inspired chef all rolled into one.' He lifted his glass in a silent toast and went on, 'Well, maybe *you'd* like to tell it, Mrs Preston?'

The housekeeper clasped her hands together and faced Liz. 'I did ring Mr Hillier a couple of days ago because I knew he'd understand.' She stopped to cast her boss an affectionate glance. 'I'm getting on a bit now,' she went on to Liz, 'and I'd really like to concentrate on my cooking. I've always liked to choose my own fresh ingredients, but for the rest of the provisioning of a household this size, and with the amount of entertaining we do, I'd like just to be able to write a list and hand it over to someone.'

She paused to draw several breaths and then continued, 'I don't want to have to worry any more about the state of the linen closet or whether we need new napkins. I don't want to have to worry about the hiring and firing of the cleaning staff, or counting the silver in case any of them are light-fingered, or wondering if I gave the same set of guests the same meals the last time they were here because I forgot to make a note of it. I'd rather there was someone who could co-ordinate it all,' she said a little wistfully.

Cam looked at Liz with a question in his eyes, and she registered the fleeting thought that he hadn't conjured up this job he'd offered her out of the blue—for whatever reason. It *did* exist. What also existed, she found herself thinking, was the fact that Cameron Hillier was well-loved by his staff. Not only Mrs Preston but Molly Swanson—and a few others she had met…

She swallowed a piece of melt-in-the-mouth steak and said, 'I think, whatever the outcome—my outcome, I mean—it would be criminal to burden you with all those other things any longer, Mrs Preston. This meal is one of the most delicious I've ever had.'

'Thank you, Miss Montrose.' Mrs Preston looked set to turn away, but she hesitated and added, 'Archie really took to you. He said you've got a little girl?'

'I do,' Liz confirmed. 'She's nearly four.'

'It's a wonderful place for kids up here.'

* * *

'So far, what do you think?' Cam Hillier queried as they walked side-by-side down to the stables after lunch.

There was a light breeze to temper the bite of the sun and to stir her hair, and the summery smell of grass and horses was all around as the path wound through the paddocks.

'I—I still don't know what to say,' Liz confessed.

He looked down at her. 'In case you're worried it's a glorified housekeeper position, I can tell you that you'd not only be in charge of the inner workings of the house but also the gardens—the whole damn lot,' he said, with a wave of his hand.

'Surely you'd be better off with a man?' she countered. 'I mean a man who could...well...' She looked around a little helplessly. 'Mend fences and so on.'

'A man who could mend fences in all likelihood couldn't run the house. A woman, on the other hand, with a sharp eye and the ability to hire the help she needs when she needs it, should be able to do both.' He paused and looked down at her. 'A woman, furthermore, who stands no nonsense from anyone has to be an asset.'

Liz released a long slow breath. 'You make me feel like a sergeant-major. I'm sorry I once threatened you, but you did ask for it.'

'Apology accepted,' he said gravely. 'Where were we? Yes. The house does need some upgrading. I've noticed it lately. Also there's the stable computer program.'

Liz was silent.

'It would look good on your résumé,' he said.

'Manager of the Yewarra Estate. It would look better than Temporary Diary Secretary.'

'Assuming I agreed, when would you expect me to start?'

He looked down at her wryly. 'Not before Roger comes back and you hand over to him. And you might need a few days off to get organised. Here we are.'

The stables were picturesque, with tubs of petunias dotted about, swept walkways and the earthy smell of manure combined with the sweet smell of hay on the air. They were also a hive of activity—and Liz saw what Cam Hillier had meant when he'd mentioned all the people who streamed in and out of the place. The stables had a separate entrance from the house.

The office yielded another scene. A giant of a man in his forties, with sandy hair and freckles, and 'outdoor type' written all over him, was sitting in front of a computer almost literally tearing his hair out.

He was Bob Collins, stud master, and he greeted Cam and Liz distractedly. 'I've lost it again,' he divulged as the cause of his distraction. 'The whole darn program seems to have disappeared down some bloody cyber black hole!'

Cam glanced at Liz. She grimaced, but pulled up a chair next to Bob and, after a few questions, began tapping the computer keys. Within a few minutes she'd restored his program.

Bob looked at her properly for the first time, clapped her on the back, and swung round to Cam. 'I don't know where you got her from, but can I have her? Please?'

Cam grinned. 'Maybe. She has to make up her mind.'

* * *

They were walking back to the house, not talking, both lost in their own thoughts, when his phone rang.

'Yep. Uh-huh… This afternoon? Well, OK, but tell Jim he'll have to fly straight back to Sydney.'

He clicked the phone off and turned to Liz. 'Change of plan. Our legal adviser needs to see me urgently. He's flying up in the company helicopter and staying the night. I—'

'How will I get home?' Liz interrupted with some agitation.

'I wasn't planning to keep you here against your will,' he said dryly. 'You're going back to Sydney on the chopper.'

Liz went red. 'Sorry,' she mumbled.

He stopped and rested his hand on her shoulder, swinging her round to face him. 'If,' he said, 'you really don't trust me, Liz, we might as well call the whole thing off here and now.'

She drew a deep breath and called on all her composure. 'I haven't had time to wonder about that—whether I trust you or not,' she said. 'I was thinking of Scout and my mother. I've never been away from them overnight before.'

His hand on her shoulder fell away, and she thought he was going to say something more, but he started to walk towards the house.

She hesitated, then followed suit.

The helicopter was blue and white, and the legal adviser looked harassed as he climbed out of it. The helicopter pad was on the other side of the house from the menagerie.

Liz felt harassed as she waited to board, but hoped she didn't look it. It was now late afternoon. She'd spent the rest of the afternoon in Mrs Preston's company, being shown over the house. It was impossible not to be impressed—especially with the nursery wing. There was a playroom that would be any kid's dream. All sorts of wonderful characters in large cut-outs lined the walls— characters out of *Peter Pan*, *Alice in Wonderland* and more—and many toys. There was a small kitchenette and three bedrooms…

On the other hand Cam Hillier, waiting with her beside the helipad, looked casual and relaxed. He had Archie with him, and it was obvious the little boy was delighted at this unscheduled change of plan.

'Can I think this over?' Liz said.

'Sure,' he agreed easily, and advanced towards the legal adviser. 'Good day, Pete. This is Liz, but she's on her way out. In you get, Liz.'

Is that all? Liz found herself wondering as she climbed into the chopper and started to belt herself up. Then she stopped abruptly.

'Uh—hang on a moment,' she said to the pilot. 'I forgot to ask him—can we just hang on a moment?'

The pilot shrugged rather boredly. 'Whatever you like.'

So Liz unbuckled herself and climbed out, and the two men on the pad turned back to her, looking surprised.

'Uh—Mr Hillier, I forgot to ask you if you'll be in the office tomorrow and at what time?'

'Not sure at this stage, Liz.'

Liz paled. 'But I've rescheduled some of today's appointments for tomorrow!'

'Then you may have to reschedule them again.'

She planted her hands on her hips. 'And what will I tell them this time?'

He shrugged. 'It's up to you.'

Liz took an angry breath, but forced herself to calm down. 'OK,' she said with an airy shrug. 'I'll tell them you've *gone fishing*!'

And with that she swung on her heel and climbed back into the chopper. 'You can go now,' she informed the pilot, her eyes the only giveaway of her true mental state. They were sparkling with anger.

He looked at her, this time with a grin tugging at his lips. 'That was telling him—good on you!'

'You—you find him hard to work for?'

The pilot inclined his head as he fired up the motor and the rotors started to turn. 'At times. But on the whole he's best bloke I've ever worked for. I guess we all think the same.'

'And that,' Liz said to her mother later that evening, having summed up the salient points of her day, 'is a sentiment shared by I would say his housekeeper, his stud master, and his secretary Molly Swanson. He can be difficult, but they really admire and respect him. His nephew adores him.' She shook her head in some confusion. 'I really didn't believe he had that side to him. Not that I'd actually thought about it.'

'Take it,' Mary said impulsively. 'Take the job. I say that because I see it as a career move for you. I see it as a way that may open all sorts of opportunities for you. If it doesn't, you can always come back to this. Anyway, the money alone will take a lot of the stress and strain from you. And I'll come with you!'

'Mum, no,' Liz said, and explained about the note she'd read. 'If I take it, one of the reasons I'll do it is so that you can have more of a life of your own, doing what you love and are so good at.'

Mary looked stubborn, and the argument went backwards and forwards until Liz said frustratedly, 'He may even have changed his mind by tomorrow—he can be annoying at times, and I more or less told him so today. He can certainly be an arrogant multi-millionaire.'

But when she went to bed she was thinking of Archie, and that brought his uncle into a different light for her. Arrogant Cam Hillier could certainly be—but when you saw him with his nephew he was a different man. Different and appealing…

Unaware that he'd just been categorised as an arrogant multi-millionaire, Cam Hillier nevertheless found himself thinking of Liz as he poured himself a nightcap and took it to his study. His legal adviser had gone to bed and so had Archie—a lot earlier.

She was a strange mixture, he decided, and grinned suddenly as he recalled her parting jibe on the helipad. So bright and capable, so attractive… He thought of her slim, elegant figure today, beneath her jumper and jeans, and the easy, fluid way she walked. He thought of the way she could look right through you out of those chilly blue eyes, but on the other hand how she could light up as she had over his gardens and with Archie.

He sobered, though, as he thought that there was no doubt she had a tortured soul.

No wonder, he reflected as he stared into the amber depths of his drink, and remembered with the stabbing sense of loss it always brought his sister Amelia, Archie's mother, and what single motherhood had done to her...

He sighed and transferred his attention to the paintings on his study walls—horses and trawlers and Shakespeare. And one trawler in particular, *Miss Miranda*, because it had been the first trawler his parents had bought. There was a new Miranda now, *Miss Miranda II*, much larger than her predecessor, and yet to be immortalised in paint.

He shrugged as he strolled back to his desk and sank down into his swivel chair. He found himself thinking back to his parents' early days.

They must have made an unlikely couple when they'd first married: the girl from an impoverished but blue-blooded background, and the tall, laconic bushman who'd grown up in Cooktown in Far North Queensland on a cattle station, with the sea in his veins and a dream of owning a prawning fleet.

In fact they'd made such an unlikely couple to his mother's family, the Hastings clan, they'd virtually cast her off—apart from Narelle, his great-aunt. Yet his parents had been deeply in love until the day they'd died—together. It had been a love that had carried them through all their trials and tribulations—all their hard days at sea on boats that smelt of fish and diesel and often broke down. Through days of tropical heat in Cooktown, when the boats had been laid up in the off-season, and through nights when the catch had been small enough to break your heart.

Somehow, though, his mother had managed to make wherever they were a home—even if only via a hibiscus bloom in a glass, or a little decoupage of shells, and her warm smile. And she'd been able to do that even when she must have been longing for more temperate climates, a gracious home and great gardens such as she'd known as a child. And his father, even when he'd been bone-tired and looking every year of his age and more, had always seemed to know when that shadow was not far from his mother. He'd always been able to make the sun shine for her again—sometimes just with a touch of a hand on her hair.

Cam drained his glass and twirled it in his fingers.

Why did thinking of his parents so often make him feel—what? As if he was playing his life like a discordant piece of music?

Was it because, although he'd taken the strands of all their hard work and pulled them together, and gone on to make a huge fortune from them, he didn't have what they'd had?

On the other side of the scale, though, was the memory of his sister Amelia, who'd loved unwisely and been dumped, never to be the same girl again. And now there was Archie—both motherless and fatherless because Amelia had taken the secret of who his father was to her grave.

If that wasn't enough to make one cynical about love and its disastrous consequences, what was?

He grimaced. Hot on the heels of that had to come all the women who pursued him for his money.

Funny, really, he mused, but in his heart of hearts was he as cynical about love as Liz Montrose?

He stretched and linked his hands behind his head, and wondered if the fault was with him—this feeling of discord with his life. Were his expectations of women way too high? Was that why he'd stopped even looking for his ideal woman? Was it all underpinned by the tragedy of his sister?

And in a more general sense was he frustrated because he felt he wasn't doing the right thing by Archie? Yes, he could give him everything that opened and shut—yes, he could come up with ideas like the menagerie—but his time was another matter.

He unlinked his hands and sat up abruptly as it came to him that it wasn't only Archie who needed more of his time. He himself had got onto a treadmill of work and the acquisition of more power that at times felt like a strait-jacket, but he didn't seem to be able to get himself off it.

He took up his glass and stared unseeingly across the room.

Was it all bound up with not having a permanent woman in his life or a proper family? he wondered. He set his glass down with a sudden thump at the thought.

Was that why he was making sure Liz Montrose couldn't ride off into the sunset? Because of more than a physical attraction he couldn't seem to eradicate? Did he have at the back of his mind the prospect of creating a family unit with her and her daughter and Archie? Was that why he'd broken the unspoken truce between them just before offering her a job?

He hadn't planned to do that. He'd been needled into doing it because she could be so damn cool—and he not only wanted her body, he wanted *her*.

But what if a tortured Ice Queen turned out to be the one he really wanted and couldn't have? he asked himself.

CHAPTER FIVE

L IZ WAS LATE for work the next morning—thanks to an uncharacteristic tantrum from Scout. She hadn't wanted to get dressed, she hadn't wanted breakfast, she hadn't wanted to do anything she usually did.

Since she wasn't running a temperature, and had no other symptoms, Liz had concluded that her daughter had picked up her own uneasy vibes after another restless night.

'Go,' Mary had said. 'Well, finish getting dressed first. She'll be fine with me. And remember what I said,' she'd added pointedly.

So Liz had hurriedly finished dressing, thanking heaven she'd chosen a simple outfit—the ultimate little black dress, with a square neck, cap sleeves, a belted waistline and a short skirt. She'd slipped on high-heeled taupe shoes, dragged on two broad colourful bangles, grabbed her purse and run for the bus.

She was only fifteen minutes late now, after a lightning call into the staff powder room to put on some make-up and check her hair. Therefore it was a rather nasty surprise to be told as she greeted Molly that her boss was waiting for her.

'W-waiting?' she stammered. 'I didn't think he'd be in today—well, not this morning anyway.'

'He's been here over an hour. Grab the diary,' Molly recommended.

Liz did as she was told, and, after taking several deep breaths, knocked and let herself into Cam Hillier's office.

He was on the phone and gestured for her to sit down.

She put the diary on the desk and not only sat down but tried to regroup as best she could, while he talked on the phone, lying back in his chair, half turned away from her.

She pushed her hair behind her ears, smoothed her skirt and crossed her ankles. She did some discreet facial exercises, then squared her shoulders and folded her hands in her lap and studied them.

'Ready?'

Her lashes flew up and to her consternation she realised that she hadn't noticed him finish his call. 'Uh—yes. I'm sorry I'm late.'

'But you weren't expecting me to be in?' he suggested.

'It wasn't that. Scout was a little off-colour. Mind you,' she added honestly, 'I *wasn't* expecting you to be in.'

He watched her for a long moment, his dense blue eyes entirely enigmatic. 'I decided,' he said at last, 'that my reputation might not stand a "gone fishing" tag.'

Liz coloured faintly. 'I wouldn't have done that,' she murmured.

'Yesterday afternoon you would have,' he countered gravely.

Liz moved a little uneasily and said nothing.

He got up and walked over to the wide windows that overlooked the city. Gone was the informality, clothes-wise, of yesterday. Today he wore a navy suit, with a grey and white pinstriped shirt and a midnight-blue tie. Today he looked every inch the successful businessman who'd diversified from a fishing fleet into many other enterprises.

He turned to look at her. 'So? Any decision?'

Liz licked her lips. 'Well, I've discussed it with my mother, and she—' She broke off and cleared her throat. 'No,' she amended. '*I'd* like to take the position—if you haven't changed your mind?'

He shoved his hands into his pockets. 'Why would I?'

Liz grimaced. 'Because of the "gone fishing" tag?'

He smiled briefly. 'I was being bloody-minded. I probably deserved it. No, I haven't changed my mind. Go on? I take it you'd like me to believe you and not your mother made the decision?'

'Yes,' she admitted, and smoothed her skirt again. 'To be honest, I couldn't in all conscience turn it down. Financially it would put me in a much better place. It would be like working from home, and it would mean I don't have to take part-time weekend work. Career-wise—as you said—it would look much better on my résumé. It would give me so much more time with Scout, and...' She paused and swallowed. 'Overall, I think it would make me look like a much more suitable mother—able to offer Scout much more, sort of thing.'

'If Scout's father decided to contest your suitability, do you mean?'

She nodded.

'So you're going to tell him?'

'No. But…' Liz hesitated. 'He has moved back to Sydney.' She explained how she'd come to know this. 'So that's another reason I'd be happier somewhere else.'

'You can't keep running away from him, Liz.'

She spread her hands. 'I know that. Still, I would be happier. And I think a better job like this would make me feel I had more…stature—would make me feel a lot better about myself, my life, et cetera.'

He brooded over this for a moment, then, 'And your mother? What's her opinion?'

'She's all for it—although it took a bit of persuading to get her to agree to stay in Sydney and take up the costume design job. But I pointed out that she's only fifty and she needs a life of her own. Of course she'll come up and spend time with us—if that's OK?'

'Fine.' His lips twisted. 'Are you looking forward to it, though? All the pragmatism in the world isn't going be much good to you if you hate it up there. If you feel it's beneath your skills or whatever.'

'*Hate* it up there?' Liz repeated wryly. 'That would be hard to do.'

'Or if you feel lonely.'

Their gazes caught as he said it, and Liz found she

couldn't look away. Something in the way he said it, and the way he was looking at her, held her trapped.

She moistened her lips. 'I plan to be too busy to feel lonely.'

But she knew immediately this wasn't the right response. It didn't answer the unasked question he was posing—the question of, as he had put it, the electricity that sometimes sizzled between them. Even now it was there between them as he stood watching her, so tall, so— She sought for the right expression. So dynamic that she couldn't help being physically moved by him—moved and made to wonder what it would be like to be in his arms.

She actually felt all the little hairs on her body stand up as she wondered this, and realised to her amazement that she'd given herself goosebumps again.

But there was more.

Lonely, she thought on a sudden indrawn breath.

She'd been lonely for years. Lonely for that special companionship with a man who was your lover. And she had no doubt that Cameron Hillier would meld those two roles brilliantly. For how long, though, before another Portia crossed his path? Well, maybe not a Portia, but— Stop it! she told herself. Don't go there…

'Liz? Are we going to play games about this?'

She trembled inwardly, but it struck her that she'd only ever been honest with this man, and she'd continue to be so.

'If you mean am I going to deny that an attraction exists for me? No, I'm not. But…' She paused and rubbed her palms together, then laced her fingers. 'I can't let it affect me. I made one terrible mistake in the name of what I thought was love, but it turned out to be only a passing attraction. I'm still trying to pick up the pieces—the pieces not only of my life but of my—my morale, maybe.'

She stopped, and didn't know that a terrible tension was visible in her expression. She did try to lighten her tone. 'You'd think five years would be enough to get over it.' She smiled briefly. 'But not so. And then, if you'll forgive me, Mr Hillier, there's you.'

'Go on,' he invited dryly. 'Or can I guess? You don't know whether my intentions are honourable or the opposite?' He paused, then said deliberately, 'I certainly wouldn't be so heartless as to leave you pregnant and alone.'

'I did...walk out on him,' she whispered.

'Liz, you're twenty-four now. That means you would have only been *nineteen* when it happened. Right?' he said interrogatively.

'Well, yes. But—'

'How old was he?' he continued. 'Older, I gather?'

'He—he was thirty-five.'

'And who was he? I don't want names,' he added as she took a quick, tempestuous breath. 'What was he in your life?'

Her shoulders slumped. 'One of my tutors.'

He studied her for a long moment. 'That's an old, old story, Liz,' he said. 'An older man in some sort of authority. A young, possibly naïve, starstruck girl. He shouldn't have walked out of your life without a backward glance when things came right for him with another woman. He should have known better *right from the start.*'

Liz fiddled with her bangles for a long moment and found that breathing was difficult. Why? she questioned herself. Because those had been her own bitter sentiments even while she'd changed courses and campuses and finally finished her degree as an external student?

'Look,' she said in a strained voice to match the expression in her eyes, 'for whatever reason—I mean legitimate or otherwise—I'm not ready to go down that road again.'

'Why are you taking the job, then?'

She gestured. 'It's the only opportunity that's come my way so far to climb out of the hole Scout and I are stuck in. And...' She stopped.

'Go on?' he prompted.

She moistened her lips. 'This may sound strange, but seeing you with Archie sort of—made up my mind. But if it's going to...' She hesitated.

'Going to what? Make my life uncomfortable?' he suggested.

Liz coloured. 'I don't— I mean I—' She bit her lip.

He crossed to the desk and dropped into his chair. 'Perhaps I should take up wood-chopping?' His lips twitched.

'Seriously,' Liz said quietly, 'perhaps we should forget all about it?'

He swung his chair round so he was facing her, and she could see suddenly that he was stone-cold sober. 'No. You seem convinced you can handle it, so I'll do the same.'

'I still don't quite understand why you've offered me the position if—' She stopped a little helplessly.

'If I'm not going to get you down the slippery slope into my bed?' He looked coolly amused. 'I think it's because of my sister,' he went on. 'One reason, anyway. Hers was a similar story to yours, but we never got to know who Archie's father was. She refused to say, but she was obviously traumatized. She was bitter, and she felt she'd been betrayed. I sometimes wonder if she thought I would—' he gestured '—take matters into my own hands if she told me who he was. Then she was killed on a skiing holiday in an avalanche when Archie was three, and the secret died with her.'

'Would you have?' Liz asked round-eyed. 'Taken matters…?'

Cam Hillier looked away, his mouth set in a hard line. 'I don't know what I might have done. I hated seeing her so distressed.'

'So you had absolutely no idea who he was?'

'No. She was overseas at the time.'

'Oh. I'm sorry.'

He stared past her, his eyes bleak, then he shrugged. 'So we're on, Miss Montrose?'

Liz hesitated.

'Don't worry, I won't impose on you.'

He was not to know that his promise not to impose on her had sent an irrational—*highly* irrational—shiver down her spine, although she ignored it.

'Yes,' she said at last.

'OK. I'll get things underway. Now, let's see what the diary holds for today.'

Liz hesitated, then reached for the diary and went through his appointments one by one.

At the end of it he told her what he wanted her to arrange for him in the next few days, and it was all normal and businesslike as Liz made notes. Finally she stood up, saying, 'I'll get on to it.' She turned away.

It was as she was almost at the door that he said her name.

She turned back with her eyebrows raised.

He paused, then said quietly, 'You can always talk to me, you know. If you need to—or want to.'

Liz stared at him, and to her horror felt tears rising to the surface. She blinked several times and cleared her throat. 'Thanks,' she said huskily. 'Thank you.' And she turned away quickly, praying he would not notice how she'd been affected by a few simple words of kindness...

Lying in bed that night, though, she wondered if it was that unexpected streak of kindness in him that she— loved? No—not that, surely? But it was something that drew her to him.

CHAPTER SIX

A MONTH after she'd started work at Yewarra, Liz had to concede that Cam Hillier had kept his promise.

It had been a hard-working but satisfying month. She'd settled into the cottage, which wasn't far from the house and, although small, was comfortable, with its own fenced garden. It was not only comfortable but picturesque, with some lovely creepers smothering its white walls. There was also a double swing seat with a canopy in the garden that just invited you to relax on it.

Probably because of having lived in an apartment all her life Scout loved the garden, and Liz loved the fact that when she could work from the cottage, in an inglenook converted to a small office, she could keep an eye on Scout through the window.

It also gave Liz her own freedom. Although she sometimes accepted Mrs Preston's invitation to eat up at the house, she more often cooked for herself and Scout. And when Cam was in residence and entertaining she had a place to retreat to.

At the same time—and she hadn't thought it possible—Scout was weaving her way more and more into her heart. She tried to analyse why, and decided it had something to do with she herself being under much less stress and being able to spend much more time with Scout.

They'd got into the habit of Scout coming into her bed every morning, bringing her favourite doll, Jenny Penny.

One morning Scout said to Liz, 'You've got me and I've got Jenny Penny. We're lucky, Mummy!'

'Sweetheart,' Liz responded, giving her blue-eyed, curly-haired daughter half a hundred kisses—a game they played— 'I am so lucky to have you I can't believe it sometimes!'

She *had* been aware that she'd been under discreet surveillance as she'd fitted into the job. Mrs Preston might be a motherly soul, and Bob might be a friendly bear of a man, but that hadn't stopped them from monitoring her progress—especially where Archie was concerned.

It hadn't annoyed her. It had made sense.

Mary had come up for a couple of weekends, and appeared satisfied that her daughter and granddaughter were in a good place. At the same time Liz had been happy to see that her mother was in high spirits— excited, and full of ideas for the costumes she was designing. Plus, Liz thought she'd detected that Mary might have a man in her life, from the odd things she'd let drop about how this or that had appealed to Martin.

But Liz's enquiries had only sent her mother faintly pink at the same time as she shrugged noncommittally.

Mary had also met Cam a couple of times and been visibly impressed. Not that that was so surprising, Liz acknowledged. What *was* surprising—although Mary had always been intuitive—was her mother's discreet summing up of the situation between her daughter and her daughter's employer.

She knows, Liz thought with an inward tremor. Somehow she's divined that things aren't quite as they seem between Cam and me.

Mary had said nothing, however, and Liz was more than happy to allow it to lie unspoken between them and, hopefully, to sink away into oblivion.

As for the work side of Liz's life—she'd gone through the big house and identified what needed repairing, replacing or upgrading, and she'd set it all in motion. She'd had a section of the stable driveway repaved where it had badly needed it, and she'd personally checked all the fence lines on Yewarra.

She'd done this on a quiet mare Bob had told her she could ride whenever she wanted to. She'd thoroughly enjoyed getting back into the saddle, and she loved the country air and the scenery.

Setting up a computer program for the stables had come easily to her, and had provided a source of great pleasure for Scout and Archie as she often took them with her to check out the foals born on Yewarra. They made up names for them as they watched them progress from stiff-legged newborns to frisky and confident in an amazingly short time.

There had been some moments of unease for her,

however, during the month. Faint shadows that had darkened her enjoyment and sense of fulfilment...

Don't get too used to this, she'd warned herself. Whatever you do, don't get a feeling of *mistress of all she surveys.* Don't let yourself feel too much at home because sooner or later you'll have to move on.

She'd reiterated those warnings to herself a couple of times, when Cam had been home with a party of guests, but from a slightly different angle. It was one thing to work with Mrs Preston and the household staff to make sure everything went like clockwork. It was another to watch from the sidelines and feel a bit like Cinderella.

And it was yet another again to find herself keeping tabs on her employer—no, not that, she thought with impatience. Surely not that! So what? To have a sixth sense whenever he was home as to his whereabouts? To feel her skin prickling in a way that told her he was nearby?

To—go on: admit it—feel needled by the way he kept his distance from her? How ridiculous is that? she asked herself more than once.

Then there was Archie.

A serious, sensitive little boy, with grey eyes and brown hair that stuck up stubbornly from his crown, he worried about all sorts of things—when five of Wenonah's puppies were sent to their new homes he hardly ate all day and couldn't sleep that night. And he pulled at her heartstrings at times when she thought about him being motherless and fatherless. When she could see how he hero-worshipped Cam, who tried to temper the little time he could spend with the boy by

sending him postcards and books and weird and wonderful things from different parts of the country and
overseas—things that Archie took inordinate pride in
and kept in a special cabinet in his room.

'Of course they're not all suitable for a five-year-old,'
Archie's nanny said to her once, when they were looking
through them. 'Take this.' She pulled down a full-size
boomerang from a shelf Archie couldn't reach. 'Archie
didn't realise he shouldn't experiment with it inside and
he threw it through a window, breaking the glass. He
was really upset—until Mr Hillier found him a song
about a man whose boomerang wouldn't come back.
Archie loves it. It really cracks him up and it made him
feel much better.'

'I—I know it,' Liz said with a smile in her voice, and
she thought, so that explains *that*!

She couldn't deny that she was getting very fond of
Archie.

As for Scout, although she'd missed Mary for a time,
she'd taken to Daisy Kerr, Archie's nanny, and so had
Liz. Daisy was a practical girl, very mindful of her re-
sponsibilities, but with a streak of romance and nonsense
in her that lent itself to the magical world kids loved.

And, between them, Liz and Daisy had soon joined
forces to occupy the children with all sorts of games.

One memorable one had been the baby elephant walk.
When a real baby elephant had been born at Taronga
Zoo, they'd watched its progress avidly on the inter-
net, and Liz had found a recording of Henry Mancini's
"Baby Elephant Walk" from the movie *Hatari*.

She and Daisy had mimicked elephants, and with one

arm outstretched for the trunk and one held behind the back they'd paced around the playroom to the music. Scout and Archie had quickly caught on, and it had become a favourite game.

None of them had realised that Cam was watching one day, unseen from the doorway, as they shuffled their way around and then all fell in a heap, the kids screaming with laughter. Liz had coloured at the indignity of it as she'd hastily got to her feet and patted herself down, but her boss had been laughing and she'd caught a glint of approval in his blue gaze.

Scout had been a little wary of Archie to begin with. It was plain Archie saw himself as the senior child on Yewarra, not to mention owner and architect of the menagerie. As such he dictated what they should do and what they should play.

Scout bore it with equanimity until one day, almost a month on, when Archie removed a toy from her. She screamed blue murder as she wrested it back, and then she pushed him over.

'Scout!' Liz scolded as she picked up the astonished Archie and gave him a hug.

'Mine!' Scout declared as she clasped the toy to her chest and stamped her foot.

'Well...' Liz said a little helplessly

'Like mother like daughter,' Cam Hillier murmured, causing Liz to swing round in surprise.

'I didn't know you were here!'

He straightened from where he'd propped his wide shoulders against the playroom doorframe. 'Just arrived.

I drove up. So she's got a temper and a mind of her own, young Scout?'

Liz grimaced. 'Apparently. I've never seen her react like that before.' She turned back. 'Scout, you mustn't do that. Archie, are you all right?'

Daisy took over at this point. 'You'll be fine, won't you, Archie? And we'll all be friends now. I know—let's go and see Wenonah and her puppy.'

Liz and Cam watched the three of them head off towards the stables, peace and contentment restored, although Liz felt somewhat guilty.

'Thank heavens for Wenonah and her puppy—look, I'm sorry,' she said. 'They usually get along like a house on fire.'

He shrugged. 'It probably won't do Archie any harm to learn from an early age that the female sex can be unpredictable.'

Liz opened her mouth, closed it, then chuckled. 'But you must admit I don't go around pushing people over. Or screaming at them,' she said humorously.

He glanced down at her quizzically as they walked side by side into the kitchen.

Liz clicked her tongue. 'Well, maybe I *did* threaten you once—but under extreme provocation, and I would never have carried it out! I didn't scream either.' She stopped and had to laugh. 'I would have loved to, though.'

'Oh, good. There are some things I did want to speak to you about. When would you like to have a tour?'

'I think I'm going to hit the sack after this. How about tomorrow morning?'

'Fine.' But she said it slowly and looked at him rather narrowly.

'What?' he queried.

'Are you feeling OK? I only ask,' she added hastily, 'because I've never seen you less than...well, full of energy.'

Cam Hillier drummed his fingers on the table, then raked a hand through his hair and rubbed the blue shadows on his jaw. He wondered what she would say if he told her the truth.

That he was growingly plagued by thoughts of her. That when he allowed himself to step into his imagination he could picture himself exploring the pale, satiny, secret places of her slim elegant body. He could visualise himself, with the lightest touch, bringing her to the incandescence he'd seen in her once or twice—but much more than that, more personal, more physical, more joyful.

He could see her, in his mind's eye, breathless, beaded with sweat, and achingly beautiful as she responded to his ardour with her own...

How would she react if she knew that to see her apparently blooming when he was going through all this was actually annoying the hell out of him?

That, and something else. He was the one who had visualised a family unit. He was the one who'd dug into his subconscious and realised his business life had taken over his whole life—to its detriment—but he didn't seem to be able to change gears and slow down. It had been *his* somewhat shadowy intention to see how

Liz fitted into Yewarra, and therefore by extension his life, to make it work better for him—for both of them.

Yes, he'd kept his distance for the last month, to give her time to settle in and because he'd made her a promise, but it had become an increasing hardship. What he hadn't expected was to find that the family circle had been well and truly forged—Liz, Scout and Archie—and *he* now felt like an outsider in his own home.

Was there any softening in her attitude towards men, and towards him in particular? he wondered, and was on the point of simply asking her outright. Take it easy, he advised himself instead. Don't go crashing around like a bull in a china shop. But he grimaced. He knew himself well enough to know that he would bring the subject up sooner or later...

'I'm OK,' he said at length. 'Thank you for your concern,' he added formally, although he couldn't prevent the faintest hint of irony as well. 'I should be back to fighting fit by tomorrow.' And the sooner I get out of here the better, he added, but this time to himself.

Liz might not have been privy to her employer's thoughts, but she found she was curiously restless after their encounter.

Restless and uneasy, but not able to say why.

The next morning she told herself she'd been imagining things as they toured the house and she pointed out to Cam what she'd organised for it.

He appeared to be back to normal. He looked refreshed, and his manner was easy. He also looked quintessentially at home on his country estate, in jeans and a khaki bush shirt. And he'd already—with Archie and Scout's assistance—been on a tadpole-gathering exercise in a creek not far from the house, to add to the menagerie's frog population.

Scout, who'd been a bit awestruck when she'd first met Cam Hillier, had completely lost her reserve now, Liz noted. And that led her to think, still with some amazement, about the two sides that made up her employer: the dictatorial, high-flying businessman, and the man who was surprisingly good with little kids.

'This is the only room where it seemed like a good idea to start from scratch,' she said as they stood in the doorway of the veranda lounge, which was glassed in conservatory-style, with a paved area outside and views of the valley. It was the focal point for guests for morning and afternoon tea. As such, it got a lot of use—and was showing it.

Cam had already approved the upgrading of two guest bedrooms, the new plumbing she'd ordered for some of the bathrooms, the new range she'd ordered for Mrs Preston, and he'd waved a hand when she told him about the linen, crockery and kitchenware she'd ordered.

'I got a quote and some sketches and samples from an interior decorating firm,' she told him, 'but I thought you'd like the final say.'

'Show me.'

So she displayed the sketches, the pictures of furniture and the fabric samples.

Cam studied them. 'Got a pin?'

She frowned. 'A pin?'

'Do you always repeat what people say to you?' he enquired.

'No,' she retorted.

'You seem to do it a lot with me.'

'That's because you consistently take me by surprise!' she countered. 'What on earth—?' She paused and stared at him. 'Don't tell me you're going to choose one with a pin?'

He laughed at her expression. 'It's not sacrilege, and since I don't have a wife to do it for me, what's left? Or why don't you choose?'

'Because I don't have to live with it. Because I'm not...' She stopped and stared at him as a vision she'd warned herself so often against entertaining raced through her mind.

'Because you're not my wife? Of course I know that, dear Liz,' he drawled, and once again couldn't help a certain tinge of irony.

She might have missed it yesterday, but Liz didn't miss it now. She blinked as she became aware of a need to proceed with caution, of dangerous undercurrents between them that she didn't fully understand—or was that being naïve?

Of course it was, she chastised herself. She could feel the physical tension between them. She could feel the heat...

They were standing facing each other, separated by no more than a foot. His shirt was open at the neck and she could see the curly black hair in the vee of it. She took an unexpected breath as she visualised him without his shirt, with all the muscles of his powerful, sleek torso exposed. She felt her fingertips tingle, as if they were passing over his skin, tracing a path through those springy black curls downwards...

She felt her nipples tingle and she had a sudden, mind-blowing vision of his hand on her, tracing a similar path downwards from her breasts.

Worse, she was unable to tear her gaze from his—and she had no doubt he'd be able to read what was going through her mind as colour mounted in her cheeks and her breathing accelerated. She was not to know he could also see a pulse fluttering at the base of her throat, but she did see a nerve suddenly beating in his jaw—something she'd seen before.

She swallowed desperately and opened her mouth to say she knew not what—anything to defuse the situation—but he got in first.

'You are a woman of taste and discrimination, wouldn't you say?' His gaze wandered up and down her in a way that she thought might be slightly insolent—why?

But it did help her regain some composure. 'I guess that's for others to decide,' she said tartly, and for good measure added, 'If you really want to know, I don't like any of these ideas.'

She turned to look around at the veranda room. 'It's a room to be comfortable in—not stiff and formal, as these sketches are.' She gestured to the drawings. 'It's not a room for pastel colours and spindly furniture. You need vibrant colours and comfortable chairs. You need some indoor plants. You need—' She broke off and put her fingers to her lips, realising that in her confusion and everything else she'd got quite carried away. 'Sorry. That's only my—thinking.'

He watched her with a glint of amusement. 'Do it,' he said simply.

'What?' She raised an eyebrow at him. 'Do what?'

'Liz, you're doing it again,' he remonstrated. 'Decorate it yourself, along the lines you've just described to me. I like the sound of it. I won't,' he added deliberately, 'confuse you with a wife.'

Liz opened her mouth, but Mrs Preston intervened as she came into the room.

'Liz—excuse me, Mr Hillier—I just wanted to check with you whether the barbecue is going ahead this afternoon?'

'Oh!' Liz hesitated, then turned to Cam. 'I was going to have an early barbecue for the kids—round about five this afternoon, in my garden. We've done that a couple of times lately and they both really enjoy it. But you might like to have Archie to yourself?'

'What I'd like is to be invited to the barbecue,' Cam Hillier said blandly.

'So I don't need to cater for you this evening, Mr Hillier?' Mrs Preston put in—a little hastily, Liz thought with an inward frown.

Cam raised his eyebrows at Liz.

'Uh—no. I mean, yes. I mean...' Liz stopped on an edge of frustration. 'No, you don't, Mrs Preston. Please do come to the barbecue, Mr Hillier.'

'If you're sure it's not too much trouble, Miss Montrose?' he replied formally.

'Not at all,' she said, with the slightest edge that she

hoped wasn't apparent to Mrs Preston. But she knew she was being laughed at and couldn't help herself. 'We specialise in sausages on bread.'

'Oh!' Mrs Preston had turned away, but now she turned back, her face a study of consternation. 'Oh, look—I can help out, Liz. You can't give Mr Hillier kids' food.'

'I was only joking, Mrs Preston,' Liz said contritely, and she put her arms around that troubled lady. 'I've got—let me see...' She paused to do a mental run-through of her fridge and pantry. 'Some prime T-bones, and I can whip up a potato gnocchi with bacon and some pecorino cheese, and a green salad. How does that sound?'

Mrs Preston relaxed and patted Liz's cheek. 'I should have known you were teasing me.'

'But were you?' Cam Hillier murmured when his housekeeper was out of earshot.

'What do you mean?' Liz queried.

'*Were* you teasing her? I can actually see you deliberately condemning me to sausages on bread,' he elucidated.

Liz gathered all her sketches and samples before gainsaying a reply. 'Have you got nothing else to do but torment me?'

'*You*—' he pointed his forefingers at her pistol-wise '—are supposed to be giving *me*—' he reversed his hands '—a tour of all the great things you've done or plan to do for Yewarra.'

Liz caught her breath. 'If—' she said icily.

'Hang on—let me rephrase,' he interrupted humorously.

'Don't bother,' she flashed.

'Liz!' He was openly laughing now. 'Where's your sense of humour?'

'To quote you—flown out of the window.' She stopped and bit her lip frustratedly, because the conversation where he'd used that phrase was the last thing she wanted to bring to mind. The day he'd told her that professionalism between them had flown out of the window...

She was saved by his mobile phone.

He pulled it out of his pocket impatiently, and spoke into it equally impatiently. 'Roger, didn't I tell you not to bother me? What? All right. Hang on—no, I'll ring you back.' He flicked the phone off.

'You'll be happy to know you're released for the rest of the day, Miss Montrose,' he said dryly. 'Something has come up, as they say.'

'Oh? Not bad news?' she heard herself ask.

'If you call the potential acquisition of another company via some delicate negotiations that require my expert touch bad news, no.'

Liz blinked confusedly. 'You don't sound too happy about it, though.'

He moved his shoulders and grimaced. 'It's more work.'

'Surely—surely you could cut back?' she suggested. And with inner surprise heard herself add, 'Do you *need* another company?'

'No. But it gets to be a habit. I'll see you at five.'

Liz stared after him as he strode out of the veranda room and found herself prey to some conflicting emotions. Surely Cameron Hillier didn't deserve her sympathy for any reason? But *was* it sympathy? Or a sort of admiration tinged with—? Don't tell me, she reprimanded herself.

Surely I'm not joining the ranks of his devoted staff?

She sat down suddenly with a frown as it occurred to her that the frenetic pace her boss worked at might be a two-edged sword for him. He hadn't sounded enthusiastic at the prospect of another take-over. He'd admitted it was habit-forming in a dry way, as if to say he did it but he didn't exactly approve.

Did he have trouble relaxing? Was he unable to unwind? And if so why?

She blinked several times as it crossed her mind that she was not the only one with burdens of one sort or another. She blinked again as this revelation that Cam Hillier might need help made him suddenly more accessible to her—closer. As if she wanted to be closer, even able to help.

But what about what had gone—before she'd felt this streak of sympathy for him? What about the simmering sensual tension that had surrounded them? Where had it exploded from? In the month she'd been at Yewarra he'd given no sign of it during his visits, and she'd been highly successful at clamping down on her feelings. Or so she'd thought...

So how, and why, had it escaped from the box today, over an interior decorating issue?

Not that at all. It had been the mention of not being his wife, she suddenly realised. It was the thought of *being* his wife that had raced through her mind and opened up that flood of pure sensuality for her.

She looked around, looked at the samples and sketches she'd folded up neatly, and thought of her brief to redecorate the room. But none of those thoughts could chase away the one that underlined them. Why did she feel like a giddy schoolgirl with an adolescent crush?

The barbecue, although Liz had been dreading another encounter with Cam Hillier, and was feeling tense and uneasy in consequence, was going smoothly—at first.

She'd loaded the brick barbecue with paper and wood, and ensured the cooking grid was clean. She'd put a colourful cloth on the veranda table, along with a bunch of flowers she'd picked, and she'd lit some candles in glasses even though the sun hadn't set, to add a festive note to an occasion that the kids loved.

She'd showered, and changed into a grey short-sleeved jumper and jeans, and—as she usually did on these occasions—she'd devised a treasure hunt through the garden for Scout and Archie. Something they also loved.

As promised, she'd produced steaks, potato gnocchi and a salad, as well as sausages on bread. There was also a chocolate ice cream log waiting in the freezer.

Although all set to do the cooking on the barbecue herself, when Cam arrived with Archie Liz found herself manipulated by her boss into releasing the reins after he'd taken one shrewd glance at her. He'd brought a bottle of wine and he poured her a glass and told her to relax.

She sat down in two minds at first, but the lengthening shadows as the lovely afternoon slid towards evening, the perfume from the garden and the birdsong got to her, and she found herself feeling a little better.

He was a good cook, and he handled the fire well, she had to acknowledge when the steaks and sausages were ready. Nothing was burnt, and nothing was rare to dripping blood. It was all just right. And not only Scout and Archie, sitting on a rug on the lawn, tucked in with gusto, so did she.

Then came the chocolate ice cream log, and with it an extra surprise. Liz had stuck some sparklers into it, causing round-eyed wonder in to the kids when she lit them.

'Wow! Now it's a real party,' Archie enthused. 'Don't be scared, Scout,' he added, as Scout stuck her thumb in her mouth. 'They won't hurt you—promise. Yippee!' And, grabbing Scout by the hand, he danced around the garden with her until she forgot to be nervous.

But that wasn't the end of the surprises—although the next one was for Liz. When the kids had finished their ice cream and quietened down, could even be seen to be yawning, although they tried valiantly to hide it, Mrs Preston and Daisy appeared, with the suggestion that Scout might like to spend the night in the nursery up at the big house tonight.

Scout said, 'Yes, please—pretty please, Mummy,' before Liz had a chance to get a word in, and Archie added his own impassioned plea.

So she agreed ruefully.

It was after she'd collected Scout's pyjamas and was about to head up to the big house that Mrs Preston said, 'You two relax, now. Oh, look—you haven't finished the wine!'

Thus it was that peace and quiet descended on the garden, and Liz found herself alone with Cam and with a second glass of wine in her hand. A silver sickle moon was rising, and there was a pale plume of smoke coming from the barbecue as it sank to a bed of ashes. There were fireflies hovering above the flowerbeds, fluttering their delicate wings.

She frowned, however. 'They didn't have to do that.'

He grimaced, and went to say something in reply, she thought. But all he said in the end was, 'They do get on well, the kids.'

'I guess they have quite a bit in common. They're pretty articulate for their ages—probably because they're single kids, so they get a lot of adult attention. They have that in common. I think Archie is particularly bright, actually. And quite sensitive.'

'I think he's certainly appreciated having you and Scout around. He seems…' Cam paused, then grimaced. 'I know it sounds strange for a five-year-old, but he seems more relaxed.'

'Except when he gets shoved around—but it hasn't happened again. I've asked Daisy to watch out for it.'

'They've probably established their parameters. Their no-go zones.' He glanced at her. 'As we have.'

Liz looked down at her wine and sipped it.

'What would you say if I suggested we move our parameters, Liz?'

She opened her mouth to ask him what he meant, but that would be unworthy, she knew. In fact it would be fair to say their parameters had moved themselves of their own accord, only hours ago.

'I—I thought it was going so well,' she said desolately at last.

CHAPTER SEVEN

'It is going well, Liz,' he said dryly.

'Not if we keep—' She broke off, floundering.

'Finding ourselves wanting each other? So I wasn't imagining it earlier?'

She glinted an ironic little glance at him.

'Dear Liz,' he drawled as he interpreted the glance, 'you're not always that easy to read. For example, I arrived in your garden tonight to find you in chilly mode— prepared to hold me not so much at arm's length but at one hundred feet down a hole. Or—' he paused and inspected his glass '—prepared to scratch my eyes out if I so much as put a foot wrong.'

Liz sat up with a gasp. 'That's not true!'

He shrugged. 'Uptight, then. Which made me wonder.'

She subsided.

He watched her thoughtfully. 'Don't you think it's about time you admitted you're human? That you may have had good cause to freeze off any attraction under the weight of the betrayal you suffered but you can't go through the rest of your life like that?'

'So...so...' Her voice shook a little. 'You think I'm being melodramatic and ridiculous?'

'I didn't say that, but it is a proposition I'm putting to you. Take courage is what I'm really trying to say.'

'By having an affair with you?' She said it out of a tight throat. 'I—'

'Liz, I'm not going to get you pregnant and desert you,' he said deliberately. 'But we can't go on like this. *I* can't go on like this. I want you. I know I said I wouldn't but—' He stopped frustratedly.

'It will spoil everything, though.'

'Why?'

She licked her lips. 'Well, it would have to be sort of clandestine, and...'

'Why the hell should it be? You're probably the only one around here who doesn't believe it might be on the cards.' He lifted an ironic eyebrow at her. 'Why do you think we've been left alone in a romantically moonlit garden?'

Liz's eyes widened. 'You mean Mrs Preston and Daisy...?'

He nodded. 'They've both given me to understand you and I would be well-suited.'

'In so many words?' Liz was stunned.

He shook his head and looked amused. 'But they never lose an opportunity to sing your praises. Bob's the same. Even Hamish.' Hamish was the crusty head gardener. 'He has allowed it to pass his lips that you're "not bad for a lass". Now, that's a *real* compliment.'

Liz compressed her lips as she thought of the gossip that must have been going on behind her back.

'And Scout and Archie are too young to be affected,' he went on. 'If you're happy to go on in your job there's no reason why you shouldn't.'

Liz got up and paced across the lawn, with her arms folded, her glass in her hand.

He watched her in silence.

She turned to him at last, her eyes dark with the effort to concentrate.

'Liz,' he said barely audibly, 'let go. For once, just let go. The last thing I want to do is hurt you.' He put his glass down on the lawn and got up. 'Give me that.' He took her glass from her and put it down too. Then he put his hands around her waist loosely, and drew her slowly towards him.

Liz stiffened, but as she looked up into his face in the moonlight she suddenly knew she couldn't resist him. She raised her hand tentatively and touched her fingertips to the little lines beside his mouth—something she realised she'd wanted to do for ever, it seemed. Just as she'd wanted to be drawn to the flame of this tall, dangerously alive, incredibly exciting and tempting man for ever...

He turned his head and kissed her fingers, ran his hands up and down her back, then down to the flare of her hips. She breathed raggedly as her whole body came alive with delicious tremors.

He bent his head and started to kiss her.

Some minutes later, he picked her up and carried her to the swing seat, sat down with her across his lap.

'Forgive me,' he said then, 'but I've been wanting to do this for some time. And so have you, I can't help feeling. Maybe that's all we should think of?' And he cupped her cheek lightly.

Liz was arrested, with her lips parted, her eyes huge. And if she thought she'd been affected by him on a hot Sydney pavement, in his car, in his office, in his veranda room it was nothing to the mounting sensations she was experiencing now, in his arms.

She could literally feel her body come alight where it was in contact with his. She felt, to her astonishment, a primitive urge to throw her arms round his neck and surrender her mouth, her breasts, her whole body to him, to be played in whatever key he liked. But what she would really like, she knew, would be for him to mix his keys. To be gentle, although a little teasing, to be strong when she needed it, to be in charge when she was about to explode with desire—because she just knew he could do that to her...make her ignite.

She groaned and closed her eyes, and when she felt his mouth on hers she did put her arms around his neck and draw him closer.

He did just as she'd wished, as if he'd read her mind. He ran his fingers through her hair, then down her neck and round her throat, and that was nice. It made her skin feel like silk. But when he slipped his hand beneath her jumper and beneath her bra strap it was more than nice. It was exquisite. And tremors ran up and down her because it was almost too much to bear.

As if he sensed it, he removed his hand and stopped kissing her briefly to say, 'This can be a two-way street.'

A smile curved her lips, and she freed her hands and slid them beneath his shirt.

It was glorious, she found. A glorious warmth that came to her as she held him close. It was a kinship that banished the lonely years—but a kinship with an exciting, dangerous edge to it, she thought. A blending of their bodies—a transference, as his hands moved on her and hers moved on him, of lovely sensations and rhythms that had to lead to the final act they both not only sought but needed desperately.

But that was where the danger lay, she knew. Not only because of the consequences that could arise—she would never allow that to happen to her again—but could she afford the less tangible consequences? The giving of her soul into a man's keeping with this act, only to have it brutally returned to her?

She faltered in his arms.

He raised his head. 'Liz?' Then he smiled down at her. 'Not an Ice Queen at all. The opposite, if anything. I—'

But he never did get to say it, because she freed herself and fell off his lap.

'Liz!' He reached for her. 'What's wrong?'

She scrambled up, evading his hands and smoothing her clothes. 'You make it sound as if I'm in the habit of doing this.'

'I didn't say that.'

'You didn't have to.' She dragged her fingers through her hair.

'Liz.' He pushed himself off the swing seat and towered over her. 'You are being ridiculous now. Look, I know you might have cause to be sensitive about what men think of you, but—'

'Oh, I *am*.' She retreated a few steps. 'Sorry, but that's me!'

'Despite the fact you light up like a firecracker in my arms? No,' he said as she gasped, 'I'm *not* going to sugar-coat things between us just because you had one lousy experience.'

'Sugar-coating or not, you'll be talking to yourself. I'm going in!' And she ran across the dew-spangled lawn and into the house.

He made no attempt to follow her.

The next morning she studied herself in the bathroom mirror and flinched.

There were dark shadows under her eyes, she was pale, and she looked—not to put too fine a point on it—tormented.

She took a hot shower and dressed in navy shorts and a white T-shirt. She didn't even have Scout to distract her, she thought dismally, as she made coffee and poured herself a mug. But coffee would help, she assured herself as she picked up the phone that had a direct line to the house. Help her to do what she knew she had to do.

Two minutes later she waited for Mrs Preston to put the house phone down, then she slammed hers into its cradle and wouldn't have given a damn if it never worked again.

She took her coffee to the kitchen table, and to her horror found herself crying again. She licked the salty tears from her lips and forced herself to sip her coffee as she wondered what to do.

Her plan had been to offer her resignation to Cameron Hillier via the telephone, and not take no for an answer. That was not possible, however, because according to Mrs Preston he'd driven away from Yewarra last night.

Had he left any messages? Any instructions? Had he said when he'd be back? No, no and no, had been Mrs Preston's response. All he'd left was a note, telling her what he'd done. There'd been a puzzled note in Mrs Preston's voice—puzzled and questioning at the same time. Liz had understood, but had had no answer for her.

Typical of the arrogant man she knew him to be, she thought bitterly. How could he not know that with one short observation he'd made her feel cheap last night? How could he not know that, for her, when she gave herself to a man it could never be just sex? It was a head over heels, all bells and whistles affair for her. It was the way she was made and it had taken one awful lesson to teach her that.

On the other hand, was he entitled to be angry with her? Had she overreacted?

She paused her thoughts and got up to look out of the kitchen window. It was an overcast morning, as grey as she felt. Not only grey, but down in the dumps and… hopeless.

What if she'd said yes? Would she have spent her life feeling as if she was treading on eggshells in case it didn't last and he turned to some other woman? After all, despite his explanation of the situation that had developed between him and Portia Pengelly, she couldn't help feeling a streak of sympathy for Portia.

She also flinched inwardly because she knew herself well enough to know that she might *never* feel safe with a man again, despite the irrationality of it. It too was the way she was made. No half-measures for Liz Montrose, she thought grimly. Could she change?

But even if she did there was something holding her back—something she couldn't quite pin down in her mind. Unless…?

She stared unseeingly out of the window and thought suddenly, *Of course!* It was her reputation that was troubling her so deeply. Living with a man in an informal relationship, as opposed to Scout's father who was solidly married—could she ever feel right about that? Not so much not right, but secure in her position as the most suitable parent for Scout?

She folded her arms around her, trying desperately to find some comfort and some solution.

If she didn't agree to move in with Cam Hillier, what on earth was she going to do? Walk away? Uproot Scout? Leave Archie? Go back to living with her mother— who definitely had a man in her life and was loving every minute of it, as well as her costume-designing project?

But how could she stay…?

She reached for the other phone, the one with an outside line, and rang Cam Hillier's mobile. She couldn't allow things to simply hang, but perhaps she could offer him a week's notice so as not to destabilise his house-hold completely?

What she got was a recorded message advising callers that he was unavailable and they should contact Roger Woodward if the matter was urgent. It wasn't even his own voice. It was Roger's.

She pressed her lips together as she put the phone down, and thought, *All right!* She had no choice but to go on as usual—for the time being.

Several days later Cam stared around his office in the Hillier Corporation's premises and knew he was in deep trouble.

He'd just signed the final document that had acquired him another company and he couldn't give a damn. Worse than that, he hated the drive within him that had seen him add another burden to his life—a life that was already overburdened and completely unsatisfactory.

He'd been more right than he knew when he'd posed that question to himself—what if a tortured Ice Queen was the one woman he really wanted and couldn't have?

What if?

He'd turn into a more demented workaholic than ever. He'd turn into a monster to work for. He'd...

He threw his pen down on the desk and ground his teeth. There had to be a way to get through to Liz. He knew now they set each other alight physically—it certainly wasn't one-sided—but how to make her see there was so much more they could share? How to make her see he needed her?

He shrugged and thought with amazement that Liz Montrose had planted herself in his heart probably from the moment he'd caught her climbing over his wall. That was the way it had happened, and he was helpless to change it.

And the irony was she loved Yewarra and Archie, and Scout loved...

He sat up suddenly. Archie and Scout—would they get through to Liz where he had failed?

He came back with a house party.

It was an impromptu party in that it had somehow been missed in both his office and the Yewarra diary until it was too late cancel. And Liz and Mrs Preston had only had a couple of hours and their work cut out to have everything ready for six overnight guests.

As for her own *contretemps*—how she was going to face Cam Hillier—Liz had no idea. But she comforted herself with the thought that at least she could stay very much in the background, as she usually did when there were guests.

An hour before dinner was due to be served she learnt that she was to be denied even that respite.

She got an urgent call from Mrs Preston with the news that her offsider, Rose, who acted as a waitress, had cut her hand and wouldn't be able to work. Could Liz hand Scout over to Daisy for the night and take her place?

Liz breathed heavily, but she could tell from Mrs Preston's voice that the housekeeper was under a lot of pressure. 'Sure,' she said. 'Give me half an hour.'

* * *

She showered, and changed hastily into a little black dress and flat shoes.

She hesitated briefly in front of the bathroom mirror, then swept her hair back into a neat, severe pleat and applied no make-up. She thought of replacing her contact lenses with her glasses, but decided she didn't need to go to extremes.

Then she gathered up Scout, and everything she needed, and ran over to the big house. Archie was delighted with the unexpected change of plan, and proudly displayed the latest curiosity Cam had brought home for him: a didgeridoo that was taller than Archie himself.

Liz glanced at Daisy, who raised her eyes heavenwards.

'Problem is I can't play it—and girls aren't allowed to, Cam said.' Archie suddenly looked as troubled as only he could at times.

Liz squatted down in front of him and put an arm round him. Scout came and snuggled into her other side. She dropped light kisses on their heads. 'It's very hard,' she said seriously, 'to play a didgeridoo. You need to learn a special kind of breathing, and you need to be a bit bigger and older. So until that happens, Archie, what say we find out all about them? How they're made, where this one may have come from, and so on.'

Archie considered the matter. 'OK,' he said at last. 'Will you help me, Liz?'

'Sure,' Liz promised. 'In the meantime, goodnight to both of you. Sleep tight!' She hugged them both, and to

Daisy added, 'I took them for a run through the paddock this afternoon to check out the new foals, so they should be happy to go to bed PDQ!'

Mrs Preston was standing in the middle of the kitchen still as a statue, with her fists clenched and her eyes closed, when Liz got there.

'Mrs P! What's wrong?' Liz flew across the tiled floor. 'Are you all right?'

Mrs Preston opened her eyes and unclenched her fists. 'I'm all right, dear,' she said. 'It must be the late notice we got that's making me feel a bit flustered. And, of course, Rose cutting her hand like that.'

'Just tell me what to do. Between us we can cope!' Although she sounded bright and breezy, Liz swallowed suddenly, but told herself it was no good both she *and* Mrs Preston going to water. 'What delicious dishes have you concocted tonight?'

Mrs Preston visibly took hold of herself. 'Leek soup with croutons, roast duck with maraschino cherries, and my hot chocolate pudding for dessert. The table is set. I'll carve the duck and we'll serve it with the vegetables buffet-style on the sideboard, so they can help themselves. Could you be a love and check the table, Liz? Oh, and put out the canapés?'

'Roger wilco!'

The dining room looked lovely. The long table was clothed in cream damask with matching napkins, and a centrepiece of massed blue agapanthus stood between two silver-branched candlesticks.

Liz did a quick check of the cutlery, the crystal and

the china and found it all present and correct, then carried the canapé platters through to the veranda room. There were delicate bites of caviar—red and black—on toast, and anchovies on biscuits. There were olives and small meatballs on toothpicks, with a savoury sauce in a fluted silver dipping dish. A hot pepperoni sausage had been cut into circles and was accompanied by squares of cool Edam. There were tiny butterfly prawns with their tail shells still attached, so they could be dipped into the thousand island sauce in a crystal bowl.

It was the prawns that reminded Liz of the need for napkins for the canapés. She found them, and jogged back to the veranda room—not that they were running late, but she had the feeling that the less time Mrs Preston was left alone tonight, the better.

She deployed the napkins and swung round—to run straight into Cam Hillier.

'Whoa!' he said, and steadied her with his hands on her shoulders, as he'd done once before on a hot Sydney pavement—an encounter that seemed like a lifetime away as it flashed through Liz's mind.

'Oh!' she breathed, and then to all intents and purposes was struck dumb, as the familiar sensations her boss could inflict on her ran in a clamouring tremor through her body.

'Liz?' He frowned, giving no indication that he was at all affected as she was. 'What are you doing?'

'Uh…' She took some quick breaths. 'Hello! I'm filling in for Rose. She had an accident—she cut her hand.'

His gaze took in her pinned-back hair and moved

down her body to her flat shoes. 'You're going to waitress?'

She nodded. 'Don't worry,' she assured him, 'I don't mind! Mrs Preston really needs a hand and—'

'No,' he interrupted.

Liz blinked. 'No? But—'

'No,' he repeated.

'Why not?' She stared up at him, utterly confused. He was wearing a crisp check shirt open at the throat, and pressed khaki trousers. She could smell his faint lemony aftershave, and his hair was tidy and slightly damp.

'Because,' he said, 'you're coming to this dinner as a guest.'

He removed his hands from her shoulders and with calm authority reached round her head to release her hair from its pins, which he then ceremoniously presented to her.

Liz gasped. 'How...? Why...? You can't... I can't do that! I'm not dressed or anything.' She stopped abruptly with extreme frustration. What she wore could be the least of her problems!

'You *are* dressed.' He inspected the little black dress. 'Perhaps not Joseph's amazing coat of many colours, but it'll do.'

Her mouth fell open—and Daisy walked into the veranda room, calling her name.

'There you are, Liz! Oh, sorry, Mr Hillier—I was looking for Liz to tell her that she was right. Both Archie and Scout are fast asleep!'

'That's great news, Daisy,' Cam said. 'Daisy, I have

a huge favour to ask of you,' he added. 'We seem to be short-staffed—would you mind helping Mrs Preston out with dinner tonight? Liz was going to, but I'd like her to be a guest.'

Daisy's eyes nearly fell out on stalks, but she rallied immediately. 'Of course I wouldn't mind. But…' She trailed off and looked a little anxiously at Liz.

'I look a mess?' Liz said dryly.

'No, you don't!' Daisy said loyally. 'You always look wonderful. It's just that your hair needs a brush! I'll get one.' And she twirled on her heels and ran out.

Leaving Liz confronting her employer with a mixture of sheer bewilderment and disbelief in her eyes.

'Why are you doing this?' she asked, her voice husky with surprise and uncertainty.

'Because if you ever do agree to live with me, Liz Montrose, I'd rather not have it bandied about that you were once one of my kitchen staff. For your sake, that is. *I* don't give a damn.'

Five minutes later, with her hair brushed but still no reply formulated to what her boss had said to her, Liz was being introduced to the house guests as his estate manager.

Half an hour later she was seated on his right hand, with her spoon poised to partake of Mrs Preston's pale green leek soup that was artistically swirled with cream.

It was going amazingly well, this dinner party that she had gatecrashed.

The guest party comprised two middle-aged couples,

a vibrant woman in her early thirties, and Cam's legal adviser in an unofficial capacity. The talk was wide-ranging as the duck with its lovely accompaniment of glowing maraschino cherries was served, and Liz was gradually able to lose her slightly frozen air.

And then the talk became localised—on horses. On breeding, racing, and buying and selling horses.

Thanks to the computer program Liz had set up for Bob, and her involvement in the stables, it wasn't all double Dutch to her. She was even able to describe several of the latest foals that had been born in the past few weeks.

That was when she realised that all the guests had come to view the latest crop of yearlings Yewarra had bred.

It grew on Liz that the vibrant woman—her name was Vanessa—with her golden pageboy hair, her scarlet lips and nails, her trim figure and toffee-coloured eyes, was a little curious about her. Twice she had surprised those unusual eyes resting on her speculatively.

And twice Liz had found herself thinking, *If you're wondering about me in the context of Cam Hillier, Vanessa, that's nothing to my utter confusion on the subject! But what are you doing here? A new girlfriend? No, that doesn't make sense. But...*

Finally the evening came to an end, and all the guests went to bed.

Liz retreated to the kitchen, to find it empty and gleaming. She breathed a sigh of relief and poured herself a glass of water. Daisy had obviously been a tower of strength in the kitchen tonight.

Something prompted her to go out through the kitchen door and wander through the herb garden that was Mrs Preston's pride and joy until she came to the lip of the valley.

It was only a gradual decline at that point, but it was protected by a low hedge and was an amazing spot to star-gaze. There was even a bench, and she sank down onto it and stared upwards, with her lips parted in amazement at the heavenly firmament above her.

That was how Cam Hillier found her.

'One of my favourite spots, too,' he murmured as he sat down beside her. 'I was looking for you. Put your glass down,' he instructed.

Liz opened her mouth to question this, but did as she was told instead, and he handed her a glass of champagne.

'You hardly had a mouthful of wine at dinner, and there's a refreshing quality to a glass of bubbly at the end of the day. Cheers!' He touched his glass to hers.

'Cheers,' Liz repeated, but sounded notably subdued—which she was. Subdued, tired, and entirely unsure how to cope with Cam Hillier.

'What's up?' he queried.

Liz took a large sip. 'Brrr…' She shook her head, but found her tongue suddenly loosened. 'Up? I don't know. I have no idea. If you were to ask me what's going on I wouldn't be able to tell you. I'm mystified. I'm bothered and bewildered. That's what's up,' she finished.

He laughed softly. 'OK, I'll tell you. We got into a verbal stoush the last time we met.'

She made a slight strangled sound.

He stopped, but she said nothing so he went on. 'Yes, a war of words after a rather lovely interlude, when I made an unfortunate remark which incensed you and you slammed your way inside, whilst I slammed my way back to Sydney in the dead of night, where I remained, incensed, for some days.'

He paused and went on with an entirely unexpected tinge of remorse, 'I don't very often get said no to— which may account for my lack of graciousness or my pure bloody-mindedness when it does happen. What do you think?'

'I...' Liz paused, then found she couldn't go on as a lone tear traced down her cheek. She licked the saltiness off her upper lip.

'I mean,' he went on after a long moment, 'would I be able to mend some fences between us?'

'I can't...I can't move in with you,' she said, her voice husky with emotion. 'Surely you must see that?'

'No, I don't. Why not?'

'I'd...' She hesitated, and breathed in the scent of mint from the herb garden, 'I wouldn't feel right. Anyway—' She stopped helplessly.

'Liz, surely by now you must appreciate that you have a rather amazing effect on me?'

'You don't show it.' It was out before she could help herself.

'When?'

'Earlier. When we first met.' She clicked her tongue, because that wasn't what she'd meant or wanted to say, and moved restlessly. 'I even wondered if you'd brought Vanessa up here to...to taunt me.'

'Much as I don't mind the thought of you being jeal-ous of Vanessa,' he said dryly, 'she's happily married to a champion jockey who rarely socialises on account of his weight battles.'

Liz flinched. 'Sorry,' she murmured.

'Have another sip,' he advised. 'What would you do if I told you that, along with wanting to stick pins into an Ice Queen effigy, I haven't been able to sleep. I've been a monster to work with. I kept thinking of how good you felt in my arms. I kept undressing you in my mind. Incidentally, how have *your* few days been?'

Liz swallowed as she recalled her days—as she thought of how she'd exchanged the swings for the roundabouts in her emotions. Round and round, up and down she'd been, as she'd alternated between maintain-ing her anger and wondering if he was right. Was it time to let go of her past and try to live again? Was she being unnecessarily melodramatic and tragic? But of course that hadn't been all she'd grappled with over the week.

There'd been memories of the pleasure he'd brought to her, memories of the man himself and how he could be funny and outrageously immodest when he wasn't being an arrogant multi-millionaire. How he was so good with kids—the last thing she'd have suspected of him when she'd gone to work for him. All the little things she couldn't banish that made up Cam Hillier.

'I was…a little uneven myself,' she admitted, barely audibly.

'Good.'

She looked askance at him. *'Good?'*

'I'd hate to think I was suffering alone.'

For some reason this caused Liz to chuckle—a watery little sound, but nonetheless a sound of amusement. 'You're incorrigible,' she murmured, and with a sigh of something like resignation she laid her head on his shoulder.

But she raised it immediately to look into his eyes. 'Where do we go from here, though?' There was real perturbation in her voice. 'I still can't move in with you.'

'There is another option.' He picked up her free hand and threaded his fingers through hers. 'You could marry me.'

Liz stiffened in disbelief. 'I can't just *marry* you!'

'There seems to be a hell of a lot you can't do,' he said dryly. 'What *can* you do?'

She went to get up and run as far away from him as she could, but he caught her around the waist and sat her down. He kept his hands on her waist.

'Let's not fight about this, Liz,' he recommended coolly. 'You said something to me once about two sane adults. Perhaps that's what we need now—some sanity. Let's get to the basics.'

He watched the way her mouth worked for a moment, but no sound came and he went on. 'I need a mother for Archie. You need a father for Scout and a settled background.' He raised his eyebrows. 'You couldn't find a much more solid background than this.'

Liz stared at him with her lips parted, her eyes stunned.

'Then there's you.' He tightened his hands on her

waist as she moved convulsively. 'Just listen to me,' he warned. 'You've settled into Yewarra and the life here as if you were born to it. If you don't love it, you've given a very good imitation of it. Has it been an act?' he queried curtly.

'No,' she whispered.

'And Archie?'

'I *love* Archie,' she said torturedly. 'But—'

'What about us?' His gaze raked her face, and his eyes were as brooding as she'd ever seen them. 'Let's be brutally honest for once, Liz. We're not going to be a one-night wonder. We wouldn't have felt this way for two crazy months if we were.'

She licked her lips.

'And they *have* been two crazy months, haven't they? Like a slow form of torture.'

She released a long, slow breath. 'Yes,' she said at last. 'Oh, yes.'

His hands relaxed at last on her waist. He took them away and drew her into his arms. 'Maybe we need a couple of days on our own—to get used to this idea. Would you come away with me for a while?'

'What about the kids?'

'I only meant a few days, and Archie is used to that. Perhaps your mother would come up to be with Scout?'

She took a breath. 'Well…'

'Well?' he repeated after a long moment.

It occurred to Liz that one of her hurdles in this matter was getting to the core of Cam Hillier. Discovering whether she could trust him or not. Finding out what was really behind this amazing offer of marriage.

'I—if I did it,' she said hesitantly, 'I couldn't make any promises. But you've been very good to me,' she heard herself say, 'so—'

'Liz.' His voice was suddenly rough. 'Do it or don't do it—but not out of gratitude.'

She sat up abruptly. 'I *am* grateful!'

'Then the offer's withdrawn.'

She sucked in a large amount of air. 'You're not only incorrigible, you're impossible, Cam Hillier,' she told him roundly.

'No, I'm not. Be honest, Liz. We want each other, and gratitude's got nothing to do with it.'

She opened and closed her mouth several times as her mind whirled like a Catherine wheel, seeking excuses, twirling round and round in search of escape avenues. But of course he was right. There were none.

'True,' she breathed at last. 'You're right.'

His clasp on her hand tightened almost unbearably. 'Then the offer's open again.'

'Thanks. I'll—I'll come.'

He released her hand and put his arm round her shoulders.

Liz closed her eyes and surrendered herself to the warmth that passed between them. At the same time she was conscious that she'd put her foot on an unknown path—but she just didn't seem to have the strength of mind to resist Cam Hillier.

She took refuge in the mundane, because the enormity of it all was threatening to overwhelm her.

'I'm a bit worried about Mrs Preston. She got herself into quite a state tonight.'

'I'll get her some help before we go. Don't worry. You're worse than Archie.' He slipped his fingers beneath her chin and looked down into her eyes. 'In fact,' he murmured, 'don't worry about a thing. I'll take care of it all.' And he started to kiss her.

CHAPTER EIGHT

HE TOOK HER to the Great Barrier Reef three days later. He'd told her that much, but said the rest would be a surprise.

They flew to Hamilton Island, just off Queensland's Whitsunday coast, on a commercial flight. She was quiet at first—until he put his hand over hers.

'They'll be fine—the kids.'

She looked quickly at him. 'How did you know I was thinking about them?'

'It was a safe bet,' he said wryly. 'Unless you're regretting coming away with me?'

'No...'

He narrowed his eyes at her slight hesitation, but didn't take issue with it.

She marvelled as the jet floated over the sparkling waters, the reefs, the islands of the Whitsunday Passage and right over the marina, with its masts and colourful surrounds, to land. Then she discovered they were not staying on Hamilton, although they walked around the busy harbour with its shops and art galleries, its cafés. Their luggage—not that there was a lot—seemed to have been mysteriously taken care of.

Her discovery that they weren't staying on Hamilton came in the form of a question.

'Have you got a hat?' he asked, as they stopped in front of a shop with a divine selection of hats. 'You need a hat out on the water.'

'Out on the... No, I don't have one I can squash into a suitcase. Out on the water?' she repeated.

'You'll see. Let's choose.' So they spent half an hour with Liz trying on sunhats—half an hour during which the two young, pretty shop assistants got all blushing and giggly beneath the charm and presence of Cameron Hillier.

But it was light-hearted and fun, and Liz found herself feeling light-hearted too. It was as if, she thought, all the pressure from all the difficult decisions was flowing out of her system under the influence of the holiday spirit of the island.

She chose a straw hat with a wide brim, and wore it out of the shop. They stopped at a café and had iced coffees, and shared a sinfully delicious pastry. Then, swinging her hand in his, he led down to the marina to a catamaran tied up to a jetty.

Its name was *Leilani*, and she was the last word in luxury: a blend of glossy woodwork, thick carpets, beautiful fabrics, bright brass work and sparkling white paint. The main saloon was huge, with a shipshape built-in galley. The staterooms—there were three—were wood-panelled and had sumptuous bed clothing.

There were two decks—one that led off the saloon, and an upper deck behind the fly-bridge controls.

Liz was wide-eyed even before she got to see *Leilani*'s interior. A young man in whites named Rob welcomed them aboard with a salute, and showed her to her stateroom. He returned upstairs and she heard him talking to Cam, but not what was said. When she got back on the upper deck the conference was over, and to her surprise the young man whom she'd assumed was the skipper hopped off onto the jetty as Cam started the engines and untied the lines.

'He isn't coming?' she queried.

Cam looked over his shoulder as the cat started to reverse out of the berth. 'Nope.'

She blinked. 'Do you know how to handle a boat this size?'

'Liz, I virtually grew up on boats.' He cast her a laughing look. 'Of course I do.'

She chewed her lip.

This time he laughed at her openly. 'You're getting more and more like Archie,' he teased, as he turned *Leilani* neatly on her own length and headed her for the harbour mouth. 'I'll show you how to do it—but maybe not today.'

'Do you own her—is she yours or have you borrowed her?'

'I own her.'

'I'm surprised she hasn't got a Shakespearean name!'

He said wryly, 'She was already named when I got her. It's supposed to be unlucky to change a boat's name. But funnily enough Leilani was a famous racehorse. OK. I'll need to concentrate for a few minutes,' he added as they cleared the harbour entrance.

'Where are we going?'

'Whitehaven,' he said. 'We should be there in time to see the sun set. There's nothing like it.'

He was right.

By the time the sun started to drop below the horizon they'd anchored off Whitehaven Beach, Liz had unpacked, and she was starting to feel more at home.

She'd been helped in this by the fact that once Cam was satisfied the anchor was set, and he'd turned off the motors and various other systems, he'd followed her down to the lower deck and taken her into his arms.

'A difficult few days,' he said wryly.

She could only nod in agreement. They'd decided to maintain a businesslike stance at Yewarra in front of staff and children alike—even Liz's mother, when she arrived. 'It's nothing to do with anyone but us,' he'd said. 'And we'll tell them it's a business trip to do with real estate.'

'But they'll probably be dying of curiosity,' she'd responded. 'Not the children, but…'

'Would you rather I kissed you every time I felt like it?' he'd countered.

Liz had blushed brightly and shaken her head.

'Thought not,' he'd said, with a glint of sheer devilry.

In the event he'd spent quite a bit of those three days in Sydney tidying up loose ends before going away. And Liz had spent the time he was away feeling like pinching herself—because, hard as it was to remain unaffected in his presence, it was harder to feel she'd made a rational decision when he wasn't around.

The one argument she'd bolstered herself with was that she owed it to Cam Hillier to at least try to understand him. It might be close to gratitude, but she couldn't help it; she certainly wouldn't be telling him that, though.

Now, anchored off Whitehaven Beach on his beautiful boat, he put his hand on her waist from behind and swung her round. 'I'm sorely in need of this,' he said huskily.

Liz smiled up at him and relaxed against him. 'You and me both.'

He released her waist and gathered her into his arms, making her feel slim and willowy, and said against the corner of her mouth, 'No desire to fight me or call me a menace?'

Liz suffered a jolt of laughter, but said ruefully, 'I don't know where it all went.'

'All the hostility?' He nuzzled the top of her head and moved his hands on her hips.

'Mmm... Could be something to do with—I mean it's very hard to say no to a guy with a boat like this!'

He laughed down at her and she caught her breath, because in all his dark glory he was devastatingly attractive and he made her heart beat faster and her pulses race.

'Tell you what.' He kissed her lightly. 'Why don't you change into something more comfortable whilst I whip up the sundowners that are traditional in this part of the world?'

She drew away and looked down at her clothes. She

was still wearing the jeans and top she'd travelled in. 'I guess I could. It *is* warm. How about you?'

'I'm going to sling on some shorts—but don't be long. The sun goes fast when it makes up its mind to retire.'

'Just going!' She clasped his fingers, then went inside and down to her stateroom.

'A maxi-dress! You *must* have a maxi-dress,' had been her mother's emphatic response upon learning her daughter was going to Hamilton Island in the Whitsundays, even if it was on business. 'They're all the rage. I'll bring you one!'

And despite the short notice she'd done just that—a lovely long floaty creation in white, with a wide band of tangerine swirls round the hem. It was strapless, with a built-in bra, and had a matching tangerine and white scarf to drape elegantly around her neck.

Liz slipped it on and discovered the lovely dress had a strange effect on her. It made her feel as light as a feather. It made her feel flirty and young and desirable.

In fact she stretched out her arms and did a dancing circle in front of the mirror. Then, mindful of the sun's downward path, she brushed her hair, shook her head to tousle it, put on some lipgloss and, barefoot—because that seemed to fit the scene—moved lightly up to the saloon and out on to the back deck.

Cam was already there, changed into navy shorts and a white T-shirt. He was sitting with his long legs propped up on the side of the boat. On the table beside him stood two creamy white cocktails, complete with paper parasols. There was also a pewter tray of smoked salmon canapés, topped with cream cheese and capers.

'You're a marvel, Mr Hillier!' She laughed at him with her hands on her hips. 'I had no idea you were so domesticated.'

He turned to look at her, and it was his turn to catch his breath—although she didn't know it.

Nor could she know that it crossed his mind that she'd never looked so lovely—slender, sparkling with vitality, and absolutely gorgeous...

He stood up. 'I cannot tell a lie. I did make the cocktails, but Rob organised the canapés along with a catering package. You—' he held out his hand to her '—are stunning.'

She laughed up at him as he drew her towards him. 'I also cannot tell a lie. I *feel* stunning. I mean, not that I look stunning, but I feel—'

'I know what you mean.' He bent his head and kissed her. 'OK.' He released her. 'Sit down. Cheers!' He handed her the cocktail. 'To the sunset.'

'To the sunset!' she echoed, and stared entranced at the white beach so well named and the colours in the sky as the sun sank below the tree-lined horizon.

That wasn't all there was to the sunset, though. The sky got even more colourful after the sun had disappeared, with streaks of gold cloud against a violet background that was reflected in the water, and a liquid orange horizon.

There were several other boats at anchor, and as the sunset finally withdrew its amazing colours from the sky they lit their anchor lights. Cam did the same, and then went to pour them another Mai Tai cocktail.

Liz stayed out on the deck, enjoying the warm, tropical air and the peace and serenity. It was a calm night, with just the soft lap of water against the hull.

'You could get addicted to this lifestyle,' she said with a grin when he brought their drinks out, then she sat up, looking electrified, as soft but lively music piped out onto the deck. 'How did you know?'

'Know what?'

She cocked her head to listen. 'That I was a frustrated disco dancer as a kid? I haven't danced for years. Except with Scout. She loves dancing too.' She smiled and sat back. 'I feel young all of a sudden.'

'You *are* young.' He pulled up his chair so that they were sitting knee to knee, and leant forward to fiddle with the end of her scarf. 'Actually, you make *me* feel young.'

Liz looked surprised. 'You're not old. How old are you?'

He grimaced. 'Thirty-three. Today.'

Liz sat forward in surprise. 'Why didn't you tell me?'

He lifted his shoulders. 'Birthdays come and go. They don't mean much when you start to get on. What would you have done, anyway?'

She thought for a moment. 'You seem to have everything that opens and shuts—so a present might have been difficult. But at least a card.'

'To put on my mantelpiece?' He looked amused.

'No,' she agreed ruefully. 'OK, here's my last offer.'

She leant right forward and kissed him lightly. 'Happy Birthday, Mr Hillier!'

'Miss Montrose—thank you. But I hope that was only an appetiser,' he replied wryly.

Liz trembled as she saw a nerve beat in his jaw—she'd seen it before, and she knew that under the light-hearted fun there lurked a rising tide of desire. It caused her nerves to tighten a fraction—not that she was feeling like a block of wood herself, she thought dryly, but was she ready for the inevitable?

He didn't press the matter. Whether he sensed that slight nervous reaction or not, she didn't know, but he merely kissed her back lightly and handed her a cocktail."

'Finish that. Then we have a veritable feast to get through.

A feast it was: a seafood platter heaped with prawns, crab, calamari and two lobster tails. There was also a side salad, and there was white wine to go with it. It was the kind of meal to eat slowly, often using fingers and not being too self-conscious about the smears left on your glass, despite the fingerbowl and linen napkins.

It was the perfect feast to eat on the back deck of a boat surrounded by midnight-blue sea and sky—although she could just make out the amazing sands of Whitehaven Beach.

It was a meal that lent itself to talking when the mood took them, about nothing very much, and to not feeling awkward when a silence grew. Because—and Liz grew more aware of it—there seemed to be a mental unity between them.

'That was lovely,' she said as he gathered up their plates and consigned their food scraps overboard. She got up and helped him carry the plates and accoutrements back into the galley, then washed her hands.

He did the same. 'Coffee?'

'Yes, please—I don't believe it!'

He raised an eyebrow at her.

'It's eleven o'clock.'

He grinned. 'Almost Cinderella time. Sit down. It's getting a bit cool outside. I'll make the coffee.'

Liz sank down on to the built-in settee that curved around an oval polished table. The settee was covered in mushroom-pink velour that teamed well with the cinnamon-coloured carpet, and there were jewel-bright scatter cushions in topaz, hyacinth and bronze.

She looked around. There were two lamps, shedding soft light from behind their cream shades, and beyond the saloon up a couple of steps was the wheelhouse, almost in darkness, but with a formidable array of instruments and pinpricks of light. A faint hum echoed throughout the boat.

Where she sat was superbly comfortable, and she could see across to the galley where her boss—she amended that. Her lover-to-be?—was making coffee.

'I could have done that,' she said.

'I can make decent coffee.' He reached for a plunger pot from the cabinet, then a container of coffee from the freezer. 'I have it down to a fine art,' he continued. 'Same coffee, same size measuring spoon and I can't go wrong.' He took down two Wedgwood mugs, spooned the coffee into the pot, poured boiling water on and balanced the plunger on top. 'Four minutes, then plunge.'

Liz couldn't help herself. She started to laugh softly. 'So you have an identical set-up in all your houses?'

'Yep. But I only have two houses.'

'And a boat?'

'And a boat. Actually...' He assembled cream, sugar and spoons on a tray with the mugs and pot, and brought it over to the table. 'I wasn't prevaricating about the real estate aspect of this trip. I'm looking at a house on Hamilton.'

'Oh, so you're combining pleasure with a bit of business?' she teased. 'Or maybe a bit of pleasure with a lot of business?'

'Not at all,' he denied. 'I'm relying on your judgement in the matter.'

Liz sobered. 'Really? I mean—do you *need* another house?'

'Really?' He sat down and plunged the coffee, and a lovely aroma rose from the pot. He poured it and moved her mug towards her. 'Help yourself. Do I need another house? No. But at least it's not another company.'

Liz digested this with a frown. 'Are you—do you—are you happy? With your life, I mean?'

He studied his coffee, then stirred some sugar in. 'I have a few regrets. Apart from Archie and Narelle I have no close relatives left. No one to benefit from the fruits of my labours, you might say.' He shrugged. 'No one to wish me happy birthday.' He looked humorous and held up a hand. 'I don't really care about that. But

I do sometimes care—greatly—that my parents didn't live to see all this.' He looked around. 'And Amelia, my sister.'

'So…' Liz hazarded. 'Are you saying…?' She paused to gather her thoughts better.

'Do I sometimes feel like saying stop the world I want to get off? Substitute the Hillier Corporation for the world? Yes.' He shrugged.

'Why—why don't you?' she breathed.

'Liz.' He looked across at her. 'It's not that easy. I employ a lot of people. And I don't know what I'd do with my time, anyway.'

He looked across at her and she could suddenly see something different about him. She could see the stamp of inner tension on the lines of his face and in his eyes.

Then he shrugged and added, 'Perhaps there's a side of me that could never sit and twiddle its thumbs? Perhaps it's the way I'm made?'

'Perhaps not,' she said huskily at length. 'Maybe it's the way things have happened for you.' She grimaced. 'Like me.'

He opened his mouth to say something, but there was a whir as an unseen machine in the wheelhouse came alive.

She looked a question at him.

'It's the weather fax,' he said with a faint frown. 'Any change in the forecast comes through automatically.'

A smile curved Liz's lips. 'Go and have a look. I know you won't rest easy until you do.'

He raked a hand through his hair and got up. 'I will.

Contrary to what you may believe about me in a car, I'm a very cautious seaman. I'll only be a moment.'

But he was a bit longer than that, and Liz leant back in a corner and curled her legs up beside her. She fell asleep without even realising it.

Cam came back with a piece of paper in his hands and the news that they'd need to change their anchorage tomorrow because of a strong wind warning.

He stopped as he realised she was asleep, and let the sheet of paper flutter to the table as he stared down at her.

He looked at the grace of her body beneath the long dress, her hand beneath her cheek, and thought that she must be really tired. Perhaps two Mai Tais and a couple of glasses of wine had contributed? Perhaps the trauma of it all…?

His lips twisted as he pulled the table away and bent to pick her up in his arms. She made a tiny murmur, but didn't wake as he carried her to her stateroom.

He put her down carefully on one side of the double bed and rolled a light-as-air eiderdown over her.

He stood looking down at her for a minute or so. Then he said, 'Goodnight, Cinderella.'

Liz slept for a few hours, then a nightmare gripped her and she woke with no idea where she was. There were different unaccountable sounds to be heard, and the terrifying conviction that she'd lost Scout.

She thrashed around on a bed she didn't know, grappling with an eiderdown she didn't remember, and was drenched in ice-cold sweat as she called Scout's name…

'Liz? Liz!' A lamp flicked on and Cam stood over her, wearing only sleep shorts. 'What's wrong?'

'I've lost Scout,' she gasped. 'Where am I?'

He sat down on the bed and pulled her up into his arms. 'You haven't lost Scout, and you're safe and sound on my boat. Remember? *Leilani* and Whitehaven Beach? Remember the sunset?'

Shudders racked her and her mouth worked.

'Scout is safe at home with Daisy and Archie and your mother at Yewarra.'

Very slowly the look of terror left her eyes and she closed them. 'Oh, thank heavens,' she breathed. Her lashes flew up. 'Are you sure?'

'Quite sure.' He said it into her hair. 'Quite sure.'

'Hold me—please hold me,' she whispered. 'I couldn't bear it if I lost Scout.'

'You're not going to lose her,' he promised. 'Hang on.' He unwound the eiderdown and lay down with her in his arms, pulling it over them. 'There. How's that?'

Liz moved against him and found the last remnants of the nightmare and her sense of dislocation leave against the security of the warmth and bulk of his body, the strength of his arms around her.

'That's wonderful.' She laid her cheek on his shoulder. 'Do you still want to marry me?'

'Liz…?' He lifted his head to look into her eyes. 'Yes. But—'

'Then do it—please. Don't take any nonsense from

me. I can be stubborn for stubborn's sake sometimes. Don't let me go—oh! I'm still dressed!'

'Liz, stop.'

He held her close, staring into her eyes with his mouth set firmly until she subsided somewhat, although she was still shivering every now and then.

'Yes, you *are* still dressed,' he said quietly. 'I don't take advantage of sleeping girls. And I don't think we should make any earth-shattering decisions right now, either. You were over-tired, overwrought, and you got a fright. So let's just take things slowly,' he said dryly, and moved away slightly.

She flinched inwardly, because whatever she might have been one thing had become crystal-clear to her through it all. Cam Hillier was her answer. Not for Scout's sake—for her sake. He not only made her feel safe, he attracted her like no other man ever had...

'Do you mean share this bed chastely?' she said huskily. 'I don't think I can. I think I've gone beyond that. You can always claim I seduced you if—if it's not what you want, too.'

He took a ragged breath. 'Not what I *want*?' he repeated through his teeth. 'If you had any idea, Cinderella...'

'Cinderella?' Her eyes widened.

He shrugged. 'It wasn't so far from midnight when I put you to bed.'

'Damn,' she said.

He lifted a surprised eyebrow at her.

'I was planning—well, I was thinking along the lines of being a birthday surprise for you. If things fell out that way. I mean, it wasn't a set-in-concrete kind of plan—more just a thought.' She trailed off, thinking that—heaven help her!—it was true.

He was silent for so long she looked away and bit her lip.

Then he said, 'Liz, I'm not made of steel.'

She looked back. 'Neither am I,' she said, barely audibly, and laid her hand on his cheek. 'I want to be held and kissed. I want to be wanted. I want to be able to show you how much I want you. Do you know when you first brought me out in goosebumps? A few days after I started working for you, when I tripped on the pavement and you caught me. Remember?'

She waited as his eyes narrowed and she saw recognition come to them.

'So I've actually been battling this thing between us longer than you have. Think of that.'

He groaned and pulled her very close. 'Don't say I didn't put up a fight,' he warned, and buried his face in her hair.

'I knew it would be like this,' Cam said.

'Like what?'

They were lying facing each other. The eiderdown had hit the carpet, along with Liz's maxi-dress and her bikini briefs—all she'd worn under it.

Her hair was spread on the pillow and looked almost ethereally fair in the lamplight.

He drew his fingers down between her breasts. 'That you'd be pale and satiny, as well as slim and elegant and achingly beautiful.'

She caught his hand and raised it to her lips. 'I sort of suspected you'd be the stuff a girl's dreams are made of. As for these—' she kissed his hand again '—I love them. They've played havoc with my equilibrium at times. They are now.'

'Like this?' He took his hand back and traced the outline of her flank down to the curve of her hip.

She caught her bottom lip between her teeth as his hand strayed to her thigh. 'Yes, like that,' she said, as those exploring fingers slid to an even more intimate position on her body. She gasped and wound her arms round his neck as all sorts of lovely sensations ran through her.

'Cam...' she said on a breath, and all playfulness left her—because she was body and soul in thrall to what he was doing to her, and because she knew he wanted her as much as she wanted him.

She could feel them moving to the same drumbeat as their bodies blended together. She could feel the powerful chemistry between them. She could glory in all the fineness of Cam's sleek powerful body, and she did. She traced the line of that dark springy hair down his torso, as she'd pictured herself doing not many days ago. She pressed her breasts against the wall of his chest and slid her leg between his.

She was overtaken by a feeling of joy as they touched, tasted and held each other. She felt like a flame in his arms—hot and desirable, then light as quicksilver. She felt wanton in one breath and irresistible to him in the next—incandescent, and totally abandoned to the pleasure he was bringing her.

Their final union brought her close to tears as the pleasure mounted to a star-shot pitch, but he held her and guided her with all the finesse and strength and control she'd probably always known Cameron Hillier would bring to this act. So that even while she was helpless with pleasure she knew she wasn't alone. She felt cherished at the same time...

'Mmmm,' he said when they were still at last. 'That was worth the wait.'

Liz put her hand on his shoulder and kissed the long, strong column of his throat. 'That was... I can't tell you... It was too wonderful to put into words.'

He traced the outline of her mouth with one long finger and looked consideringly into her eyes. 'I could try. You, my sweet, prickly, gorgeous-all-rolled-into-one Liz, created a bit of heaven on earth for me.'

She smiled and smoothed her palm on his shoulder. 'Thank you.' A tiny glint of laughter lurked in her eyes. 'But I couldn't have done it without you.'

She felt the jolt of laughter that shook him. 'No?'

'No. And you do know I'm teasing you, don't you? Because I was utterly at your mercy, Mr Hillier.'

'Not so, Miss Montrose. Well,' he amended, 'let's split the credit.'

'Sounds fair enough,' she said gravely, but all of a sudden she sobered as it came back to her—what she'd said about marrying him.

'Liz?'

She looked up into his eyes to see that he too had sobered, and that there was a question mark in their blue depths. For a moment it trembled on her lips to tell him that she'd fallen deeply in love with him—that she probably had way back, despite everything to the contrary she'd told herself.

But a remnant of fear generated from her past held her silent. Just take it slowly, she thought. Yes, she'd done it again—given herself to a man. And it was so much more than sex for her, but—for the time being anyway—should she protect herself by being the sole possessor of that knowledge?

'Nothing,' she breathed, and buried her face in his shoulder.

They had two more days on *Leilani*.

They moved the next morning to an anchorage protected from the strong winds predicted—this time to a rocky bay with turquoise waters and its own reef.

They swam and fished. They went ashore in the rubber dinghy and climbed to a saddle between the hills, from where they could see a panoramic view of the Whitsundays. They snorkelled over the coral. They paddled the light portable canoes *Leilani* carried.

Liz almost lived in her ice-blue bikini. She wore a borrowed baseball cap when they streaked across the water in the dinghy. She donned a long-sleeved white blouse as protection against the sun, and wore her sunhat on the boat. She reserved her maxi-dress for the evening.

The one thing they didn't do was discuss marriage again.

It puzzled Liz—from both their points of view. Her

unwitting reluctance to bring the subject up, and whatever reason Cam had for not doing so either. In fact a
couple of times she caught him watching her with a
faint frown in his eyes, as if he couldn't quite make her
out. On both occasions she felt a little tremor of unease.
But then he'd be such a charismatic companion she'd
forget the unease and simply enjoy being with him on
his beautiful boat.

One thing she particularly enjoyed was seeing him
relax, and the feeling that had already occurred to her
came alive in her again—Cam Hillier needed rescuing
from himself. Could she do it on a permanent basis?
Could she find the key to making a life with him that
would be satisfying enough to ease him from the strato-
sphere he inhabited and which she had the strong feeling
he was growing to hate?

She had to smile dryly at the thought, however. Who
was to say her demons would ever let her go enough to
be able to share *any* kind of a life with him?

And then it all came apart at the seams…

He said to her, apropos of nothing, 'There's no one else
anchored here today.'

They were lying on loungers on the back deck. Liz
looked around. 'So there isn't.' Then she sat up with
a faint frown. 'You said that with a peculiar sort of
significance.'

He moved his sunglasses to the top of his head. 'I
have this fantasy.' He shrugged. 'I suppose you could
say it involves mermaids.'

Liz studied him, but he was looking out over the

water. 'Go on. What has that to do with no one else being here?'

'We could skinny-dip.'

She took a breath. 'But we're not mermaids—or mermen,' she pointed out.

'All the better, really.'

'Cam—' She didn't go on.

'Liz?' He waited a moment. 'The problem is—my problem is—I'd love to see your naked body in the water.'

Liz looked down at herself. 'It's not a hugely camouflaging bikini.'

'Still...'

She looked out over the water. It looked incredibly inviting as it sparkled under a clear sky and a hot sun. Why not?

She rose noiselessly, stepped out of her bikini, and climbed down to the duckboard where she dived into the water before Cam had a chance even to get to his feet.

'Come in,' she called when she surfaced. 'It feels wonderful.'

It did, she thought as she floated on her back, but not as wonderful as when he dived in beside her and took her in his arms.

'Good thinking?' he asked, all sleek and wet and tanned, and strong and quite naked.

'Brilliant thinking,' she conceded. 'I feel like a siren,' she confessed as she lay back in the water across his arm.

'You look like one.' He drew his free hand across

the tips of her breasts, then put his hands around her waist and lifted her up. She laughed down at him with her hands on his shoulders as she dripped all over him. Then she broke free and swam away from him.

'You swim like a fish,' he called when he caught up with her. 'And you make love like a siren—come back to the boat.'

'Now?'

'Yes, now,' he said definitely.

Liz laughed, but she changed direction obediently and swam for the boat.

He followed her up the ladder, and when they reached the deck he picked her up and carried her, dripping wet, down to his stateroom, where he laid her on the bed.

'Cam,' she protested, 'we're making a mess.'

'Doesn't matter,' he growled as he lay down beside her and took her in his arms. 'This—what I desperately want to do with you—is not for public consumption.'

'There was no one there—and it was your idea anyway.'

'Perhaps—but not this. There. Comfortable?' he asked as he rolled her on top of him.

Liz took several urgent breaths, and her voice wasn't quite steady as he cradled her hips and moved against her. 'I don't know if that's the right word for it. It's…' She paused and bit her bottom lip. 'Sensational,' she breathed.

He withdrew his hands from her hips and ran them through her hair, causing a shower of droplets. They both laughed, then sobered abruptly as they began to kiss each other and writhe against each other with desperate need.

It was a swift release, that brought them back to earth gasping. Liz, at least, was stunned at the force of the need that had overtaken them. She was still breathing raggedly as they lay side by side, holding each other close.

'Where did th-that come from?' she asked unsteadily as she pulled up the sheet.

He smoothed her hair. 'You. Being a siren.'

'Not you? Being a merman?'

'I don't think there is such a thing.'

'All the same, do you really mean that? About me being a siren? It's the second time you've—well, not *accused* me of it, but something—' she hesitated '—something similar.'

She felt the movement as he shrugged, but he said nothing. In fact she got the feeling he was somewhat preoccupied. She got the feeling from the way he was watching her that he was waiting for something...

She pushed herself up and rested her elbow on the pillow, her head on her hand. 'Is something wrong?' She slipped her fingertips over the smooth skin of his shoulder.

He stared expressionlessly into her eyes, then he said, 'You're right. We have made a mess. Let's strip the bed and remake it. But have a shower first.' He threw back the sheet and got up.

Liz hesitated, feeling as if she'd stepped into a minefield. She studied his long, strong back for a moment as he reached into a cupboard for clothes. Then, with a mental shake of her head, she got up in a few quick movements and slipped past him into her stateroom, with its *en-suite* shower. She closed the door—something she wouldn't usually have done.

He didn't take issue with it.

They remade the bed in silence.

Liz had put on a pair of yellow shorts with a cream blouse and tied her hair back. He'd also donned shorts, and a black T-shirt. The tension that lay between them was palpable.

How? Why? Liz wondered.

She didn't get the opportunity to answer either of those questions as his phone rang—it was never far away from him. It was Roger, and when Cam clicked it off she knew from his expression and the few terse questions he'd posed that it was something serious.

She clutched her throat. 'Scout?' she whispered.

'Liz, *no*. She's fine. So is Archie. But Mrs Preston had been hospitalised with heart problems. I made her promise to get a check-up when you said you were worried about her.'

Liz's hand fell away. 'Oh,' she breathed, in a mixture of intense relief and concern.

'There's more. Daisy's got the flu.'

'Oh, no! So who…?'

'Your mother has taken command, with the help of Bob's wife, but I think we should go back as soon as we can.'

'Of course.' Liz looked around a little helplessly. 'But how soon can that be?'

He was already on his mobile. 'Roger's organis-
ing a flight from Hamilton. Hello, Rob?' he said into
the phone. 'Listen, mate, I need to get home ASAP.
Organise a chopper to pick us up off Whitehaven Beach.
Come on it yourself, and you can sail *Leilani* back to
Hamilton.'

Liz's mouth had fallen open at these instructions. She
closed it but got no chance to comment.

'OK,' Cam said, 'let's up anchor. It'll take us about
half an hour to get to Whitehaven.'

'What if there are no helicopters available?'

He looked at her, as if to say, *You didn't really say
that, did you?* 'Then he'll buy one.'

'Oh, come on!' Liz clicked her tongue. 'You don't
expect me to believe that?'

'Believe it or not, Ms Montrose, it's something I have
done before.' He paused and looked around. 'Would you
mind packing for both of us?'

Liz stared at him, but she recognised this Cam Hillier,
and she turned away, saying very quietly, 'Not at all.'

She didn't see him hesitate, his gaze on her back, or
see his mouth harden just before he left the stateroom.

Liz stood in the same spot for several minutes.

She heard the powerful motors fire up. She heard
above that the whine of the electric winch and the rattle
of the anchor chain as it came up. All sounds she knew
now.

She felt the vibration beneath her feet change slightly
as he engaged the gears and the boat got underway...

She licked a couple of tears from her upper lip—
because something had gone terribly wrong and she had

no idea what it was. *Ms Montrose*, she thought. Had she gone back to that? *Why* had she gone back to that?

Why this almost insane rush to get home? Yes, when he made up his mind to do something he often did it at a hundred miles an hour—and it wasn't that she didn't want to get home as soon as possible—but *this*?

Wouldn't they be alone together any more? What about that fierce lovemaking? Where did that fit in?

She buried her face in her hands.

They got back to Yewarra after dark that same evening.

Roger had organised a flight for them on a private jet from Hamilton Island with a business associate of Cam's. The associate was on the flight, so there'd been no chance of any personal conversation. And they'd flown from Sydney to Yewarra on the company helicopter—ditto no personal conversation.

Liz was unsure whether it had been fortuitous or otherwise.

Both Scout and Archie were already in bed and asleep, but Mary Montrose was there to greet them. And she had assurances that Daisy was resting comfortably and so was Mrs Preston, although she was still in hospital.

Liz hugged her mother and Cam shook her hand.

'Thanks so much for stepping into the breach, Mrs Montrose,' he said to her, and Liz could see her mother blossoming beneath his sheer charm. 'I hope you've moved into the house?'

'Yes,' Mary said, 'along with Scout. Although only

into the nursery wing. I guess you'll stay there too?' she said to Liz.

'Uh—actually,' Cam said, 'Liz and I have some news for you. We've agreed to get married.'

CHAPTER NINE

'HOW COULD YOU?'

They were in his study with the door closed. It was a windy night, and she could hear trees tossing their branches and leaves outside, as well as occasional rumbles of distant thunder

Liz was stormy-eyed and incredulous, despite the fact that her mother had greeted Cam's news with effusive enthusiasm before faltering to an anxious silence as she'd taken in her daughter's expression.

Then she'd said, 'I'll leave you two alone,' and gone away towards the nursery wing.

'It's what you told me to do,' he countered, lying back in his chair behind the desk. *"Don't take any nonsense from me,"'* he quoted. *"I can be stubborn for stubborn's sake."* Remember, Liz?' He raised a sardonic eyebrow at her and picked up his drink—he'd stopped to pour them both a brandy on their way down to the study.

Despite the drink, Liz couldn't help feeling that to be back in his study, on the opposite side of his desk from him, was taking them straight back to an employer/ employee relationship, and it hurt her dreadfully.

'There's nothing wrong with my memory,' she said

helplessly, then took a breath to compose herself. 'I also remember—not that many hours ago—being all of a sudden being frozen out after we'd slept together as if we'd never get enough of each other. The last thing I expected after that was to be told I planned to marry you.'

'But you do, don't you, Liz? Because of Scout.'

Liz paled. 'But you knew,' she whispered. 'You yourself told me that you needed a mother for Archie and I needed security for Scout.'

He got up abruptly and carried his glass over to the paintings on the wall. He stared at one in particular—the painting of a trawler with the name of *Miss Miranda*. 'I didn't know I was going to feel like this.'

She stared at him. He was gazing at the picture with one hand shoved in his pocket and tension stamped into every line of his body. Even his expression was drawn with new lines she'd never seen before.

'Like what?' she queried huskily.

He turned to her at last. 'As if I've got my just desserts. As if after playing the field—' his lips twisted with self-directed mockery '—after having a charmed life where women were concerned, being able to enjoy them without any deep commitment, I've finally fallen for one I can't have.'

Her eyes grew huge and her lips parted in astonishment. 'C-can't have?' she stammered.

He smiled briefly, and it didn't reach his eyes. 'You're doing it again, Liz. Repeating things.'

'Only because I can't believe you said that. You have—we have—I don't know how much more you could want.' Tears of confusion and desperation beaded her lashes.

He came back and sat down opposite her. 'I thought it would be enough to have you on any terms, Liz. That's why I lured you into the job up here at Yewarra. That's why—' he gestured '—I played on your insecurity over Scout. Only to discover that when you agreed to marry me you had Scout on your mind, not me. I didn't want that.'

She gasped, and her mind flew back to the first time they'd made love—to their first night on the boat and the nightmare she'd had. Flew back to his initial resistance that she, in her unwisdom, had not given enough thought to.

'You should have told me this then.'

'I nearly did. I *did* tell you I wasn't made of steel,' he said dryly. 'I didn't seem able to also admit that I was a fool—an incredible fool—not to know what had happened to me.'

'What about this morning? Was it only this morning?' she breathed. 'It seems like an eon ago.'

'This morning?' he repeated. 'What I really wanted this morning was to hear you say you loved me madly, in a way that I could believe it.'

Liz let out a long, slow breath. 'What I don't understand now is why you told my mother we were planning to marry.'

He drummed his fingers on the desk. 'That was a devil riding me. But I am prepared to give you the protection of my name if you feel it will safeguard Scout from her father. It'll be a marriage of convenience, though.' He shrugged.

'Is that what you think I want?' she whispered, paper-pale now.

He raised an eyebrow. 'Isn't it?'

Her lips trembled, and she got slowly to her feet as every fibre of her being shouted at her to deny the charge. Why couldn't she say no? It's *not* what I want. Why couldn't she tell him she'd fallen deeply and ir-revocably in love with him?

Because she had no proof? Because she saw now in hindsight that the way things had played out it *did* look as if she'd been angling for marriage because of Scout?

Because she was still unable to bare her soul to any man?

'No, it's not what I want,' she said, barely audibly. 'Cam.' She swallowed. 'It's over. We'll leave first thing tomorrow morning. It—it could never have worked be-tween us. Too many issues.' She shook her head as a couple of tears coursed down her cheeks. 'I told you once you'd be mad to want to get involved with me. I was right. Not that I blame you for the mess I...I am.' She turned away, then turned back. *'Please,'* she begged, 'just let me go.'

'Liz—' he said harshly, but she fled out of the study.

CHAPTER TEN

'WHERE'S ARCHIE?' Scout said plaintively. 'And where's 'Nonah's puppy? Why can't I play with them any more?' She looked around her grandmother's flat discontentedly. 'I don't like this place.'

Liz sighed inwardly.

It was three weeks since they'd left Yewarra—a heart-wrenching move if ever there'd been one, as she'd thought at the time.

She could still see in her mind's eye Archie, standing at the dolphin fountain waving goodbye, looking pale and confused. She could still see Cam, standing beside him but not waving, as she'd driven Scout and her mother away.

She could still remember every word of the stilted last interview she'd had with Cam, during which he'd insisted on paying her three-month contract out.

She could particularly recall the almost irresistible urge she'd had to throw herself into his arms and beg him to take her on any terms, even if she was unable to tell him what he wanted to hear. She closed her eyes in pain every time she thought of it…

She couldn't get out of her mind the thought of Cam

Hillier needing help to stabilise his life and how she was too emotionally crippled to give it to him.

In the three weeks since that parting she'd lost weight, she'd slept little, and she'd done battle with herself over and over. Had she walked away from a man who loved her for no good reason? On the other hand, would he ever trust her?

Her mother had been an absolute stalwart, doing her very best to make the dislocation more bearable for both her and Scout, but Liz knew she would have to make some changes. She couldn't go on living with her mother in the way she had. Mary was obviously very close to her new beau, Martin. She was also knee-deep in concert costumes.

But it had been a week before Liz had even been able to pull herself together and start looking for an alternative life and a job.

She'd got in touch with the agency she'd worked for and put herself back on their books. So far nothing had come up, but she had got her old weekend job as a restaurant receptionist back. Next thing on her list was a flat of her own.

It was not long after Scout had made her displeasure with their new life known that the phone rang. It was the agency, with an offer of a diary secretary position for two weeks starting the next day.

Liz accepted it after consulting her mother, although she was dreading getting back on the old treadmill. And the next morning she presented herself at a suite of offices in the city, the home of Wakefield Inc—a company that operated a cargo shipping line.

She was, she'd been told, replacing the president's diary secretary, who had fallen and broken a leg. That was all she knew.

As always for work, she'd dressed carefully in a fresh suit with a pretty top. But her hair was tied back and she wore her glasses.

She was greeted by a receptionist, whose name-plate labelled her as Gwendolyn, as she stepped out of the lift, and was ushered immediately towards the president's office when she'd explained who she was.

'In you go,' Gwendolyn said cheerfully. 'He's asked to see you immediately.'

Liz took a deep breath and hesitated. She could partly see into the office, and it looked quite different from the last office she'd worked in. No pictures of horses and trawlers that she could see, and a completely different colour scheme—beige carpet, beige walls and a brown leather buttoned settee. The desk was hidden from her, and she took another deep breath and walked through the door—only to find herself almost fainting from sheer shock.

Because it was Cam Hillier who sat behind the desk belonging to the president of Wakefield Inc—a company she'd never heard of before yesterday.

She stopped as if shot.

He got up and came round the desk towards her. 'Liz,' he said quietly. 'Come in.'

'Y-you?' she stammered. 'I don't understand.'

He smiled briefly. 'It's the company I bought while you were up at Yewarra. Remember?'

Her eyes were huge and her face was pale as her lips

worked but no sound came. She stared at him. He was formally dressed, in a navy suit she recognised. He was as dynamic and attractive as he'd ever been—although she thought he looked pale too.

'I—I don't understand,' she repeated. 'I'm supposed to be temping for someone who's broken a leg.'

'I made that up. I also asked for you personally.'

She blinked. 'You...you got me here deliberately? Why?' she asked hoarsely.

'Because I can't live without you. I need you desperately, Liz.' He put a hand out as she rocked on her feet, and closed it around her arm to steady her. 'Archie can't live without you. None of us can. So we'd be grateful for anything you can give us, but you have to come back.'

'Anything?' she whispered.

And whether it was the shock of seeing him again when she'd never expected to, or the shock of discovering he'd sought her out, it was as if some unseen hand had turned a key in her heart and everything she'd longed to say but been unable to came pouring out...

'Don't you understand? I would never have slept with you if I didn't love you. That's the way I'm made. I know—I know it looked as if it was all about Scout, but it wasn't. It was *you*. It was you from way back.'

Tears were pouring down her cheeks and she was shaking.

'Liz.' He put his arms around her, and despite her tears she could see that he was visibly shaken too, 'Liz, my darling...'

'I don't know why I couldn't say this before,' she wept. 'I *wanted* to, but—' She couldn't go on.

'I understand. I always understood,' he said softly. 'I just couldn't help myself from rushing my fences at times.'

'I'm surprised you don't hate me,' she said, distraught.

His lips twisted. 'Maybe this will reassure you more than any words,' he murmured, and took off her glasses. He started to kiss her—her tear-drenched cheeks, her brow and her mouth.

When they finally drew apart Liz was breathless, but her tears had stopped and she looked up at him in wonderment. 'It—it *is* real,' she said tentatively.

'I really love you,' he said. 'I've never felt this way before. As if I'm finally making the right music. As if the rest of the world can go to hell so long as I have you.'

He traced the outline of her swollen mouth with his forefinger. 'I never told you this—I've never told anyone this—but my parents were soul mates, and I've been looking for my soul mate for a long time. So long I didn't think it was going to happen. Until I met you.'

Liz moved in his arms. 'I had no idea.'

'Remember when you offered to take me apart?' he asked, with a wryly lifted eyebrow.

'I didn't! Well—' she shook her head '—if you say so.'

He grinned. 'That was when the danger bells started to ring for me. Although, to be honest—' he looked rueful '—when you climbed over my wall I had an inkling there could be something special about you.'

Liz gasped. 'But...'

He shrugged. 'Don't ask me why. I guess it's the way these things happen. But by the time I got you to Yewarra it was more than danger bells. It was the growing conviction that you and you alone were going to be that special one for me—if only I could get you to see it—if only I could get you to trust me.'

Liz closed her eyes and rested her head on his shoulder. 'I'm sorry.'

He kissed her lightly, then took her hand and drew her over to the buttoned settee, where they sat down with their arms around each other.

'Don't be sorry,' he said. 'Marry me instead.'

Liz laid her cheek on his shoulder. 'I can't think of anything I would rather do, but—' she sat up suddenly, and looked into his eyes with a tinge of concern in her own '—I do know I can be difficult—'

'So do I,' he interrupted. 'I've seen it. Outspoken, for example. Fighting mad at times. However, since I'm such a model of patience, so easy-going, so tolerant, so predictable, et cetera, we should complement each other.'

'Patient? Tolerant? Predictable?' Liz stared at him in disbelief, then she started to laugh. 'For a moment I thought you actually believed that,' she gurgled. 'Oh, Cam, you can be totally unpredictable, intolerant and impatient, but you can also be—in lots of ways—my hero, and I love you so very much!'

He held her as if he'd never let her go. And the magic started to course through her—the assault on her senses, the thrilling, magnetic effect he'd had on her almost from the beginning claimed her.

They could have been on the moon, she thought, as they revelled in each other. It was as if the world had melted away and all that mattered was that they'd found each other.

It was when they finally drew apart that Cam said, 'We need to get out of here.'

'Yes.' Liz pushed her hair back—he'd taken it down, and there were clips scattered she knew not where. 'Yes. But it might look—funny.'

'No, it won't.' He helped her to her feet and patted her collar down. 'Well, you did come in looking all Ice Queen, but now you look gorgeous so I don't suppose anyone will mind.'

'Cam,' she breathed, as colour came into her cheeks, but said no more as he kissed her, then took her hand and led her to the door—and once more demonstrated how unpredictable Cameron Hillier could be.

There were several people in the reception area, grouped around the reception desk. They all greeted Cam with the deference that told Liz they were employees.

He returned the greetings and rang for the lift then said to Gwendolyn, 'Gwen, may I introduce you to my future wife? This is Liz. Oh, and by the way, I won't be in for a couple of weeks, maybe even months. If anything seems desperate get hold of Roger Woodward at Hilliers, he'll sort it out.'

There was dead silence and several mouths hanging open for a couple of seconds then Gwen shot up and scooted round her desk to shake Liz's hand as well as Cam's. 'I'm so happy for you both!' she enthused. 'Not that I realized—or knew anything about it—still, all the very best wishes!' And she pumped Cam's hand again.

Another devoted employee in the making, Liz thought wryly but she was warmed as everyone else shook hands and they finally stepped into the lift.

'Poor Roger,' she said as they descended to the car park.

Cam looked surprised.

'He'll probably be tearing his hair out soon. I know the feeling,' she explained.

He took her hands. 'I apologize for all my former sins,' he said gravely. 'But there was one thing I nearly did that I narrowly, very narrowly, restrained myself from doing.'

She looked up at him expectantly.

'This.' He took her in his arms then buried a hand in her hair and started to kiss her.

They didn't notice the lift stop or the doors open, they noticed nothing until someone clearing their throat got through to them.

They broke apart to discover they had an audience of four highly interested spectators, one of them with his finger on the open button.

'Different lift but that's exactly what I wanted to do,' Cam said to her then taking her hand again led her out into the car park, adding to the small crowd, 'Forgive us but we've just agreed to get married.'

And their little crowd of spectators burst into spontaneous applause.

Liz was pink-cheeked but laughing as they made their way to the Aston Martin. Laughing and full of loving.

They flew up to Yewarra the next morning. Mrs Preston and Daisy were there to greet them, both with tears in their eyes. Bob and his wife were at the helipad—even Hamish the head gardener was there. But it was Archie who really wrung Liz's heartstrings.

He hugged Cam first, then he hugged Scout but he stood in front of Liz looking up at her with all the considerable concern he was capable of and said, 'You won't go away again, will you, Liz? You won't take Scout away again, will you? 'Cause nothing feels the same when you're not here.'

Liz sank down on her knees and put her arms around Archie and Scout. 'No. We won't go away again, I promise.'

Archie stared into her eyes for a long moment and then, as if he'd really received the reassurance he wanted, he turned to Scout. 'Guess what, Golly and Ginny have had more kids! Want to see them?'

Scout nodded and they raced off together towards the menagerie.

Liz rose to her feet and Cam took her hand. 'Thanks,' he said huskily. 'Thanks.'

They were married on Whitehaven Beach several weeks later.

Liz and Cam, with Archie and Scout and the marriage celebrant, arrived by helicopter. The guests had set out on *Leilani* and another boat from Hamilton Island earlier and were ferried to the beach by tender.

The bride wore a dress her mother had made, a glorious strapless gown of ivory lace and tulle and she had flowers woven into her hair. The bridegroom wore a cream suit. Scout and Archie both wore sailor suits. Everyone was shoeless.

Mary Montrose couldn't have looked happier. Narelle Hastings with bronze streaks in her hair to match her outfit looked faintly smug and she mntioned several times to anyone who'd listen that she'd known this was on the cards right from the beginning. Daisy and Mrs Preston were tearful again but joyfully so. So was Molly Swanson. Even Roger Woodward upon whose shoulders the organization of this unusual wedding had fallen looked happy and uplifted.

Although, he still had to get everyone safely back to Hamilton apart from the wedding party, he reminded himself, and who would have thought Cameron Hillier and Lizbeth Montrose would be so unconventional?

He clicked his tongue then had to smile as he recalled their faces when they'd told him what they wanted. They'd both been alight with love and laughter.

And now, as the sun sank, they were pronounced man and wife and as a hush fell over the guests, they stared into each other's eyes and it was plain to see that at that moment they only existed for each other as the sky turned to liquid gold and so did the water.

Then the spell was broken and the business of ferrying everyone back to *Leilani*, where a feast awaited them, began.

* * *

Several hours later, Cam and Liz farewelled their guests, who were returning to Hamilton Island on the second boat, all but two that was. Archie and Scout, both asleep now, would stay with them as they cruised the Whitsundays for the next couple of weeks.

They stood side by side as the second boat identifiable by its running lights negotiated the Solway Passage and disappeared from sight. All the guests were to spend two nights at the resort on Hamilton.

'So,' Cam put an arm around her, 'it went well. Even Roger managed to enjoy himself.'

Liz gurgled with laughter. 'Poor Roger! Yes, it went well.' She leant against him. 'Do you feel married?'

He looked down at her somewhat alarmed. 'Don't you?'

'I do.' She turned her face up to him. 'I really do.'

He cupped her cheeks, kissed her lightly, then swept her into his arms.

Twelve months later Yewarra was looking its best after good rain that had given all the gardens a boost for their final late summer flowerings.

Liz was wandering through the beds of massed roses, inhaling their delicate perfume when Cam came looking for her and he found her leaning against a tree trunk, day-dreaming.

He'd been away for a few days, and he'd just driven in. He'd discarded his suit jacket and loosened his tie and the sight of him, so tall and beautifully made, still, twelve months on, had the power to send her pulses racing.

'You're back,' she said and lifted her face for his kiss. She wore a floral summer dress that skimmed her figure, and sandals.

'You look good enough to eat,' he murmured. 'I'm not only back, I'm back where I belong.' He kissed her thoroughly then he linked his arm through hers and they started to stroll through the gardens. 'Missed me?'

She nodded but her lips curved into a smile as she thought about the changes in him. How he'd cut his work load down and what he couldn't he did mostly from home so that he was rarely gone from her, and then only for short stretches.

How he was so much more relaxed and able to enjoy their lifestyle. Not, she knew, that he wouldn't need different challenges from time to time but the frenetic pace of his previous life was a thing of the past.

As for herself, she couldn't be happier...

'How come you're so alone?' he queried as they strolled along. 'Not a kid in sight.'

'They were invited to a birthday party down the road. Daisy took them and stayed on to give a hand.'

He stopped and swung her round to face him, and frowned. 'Why do you look—I don't know—secretive?'

'Ah,' Liz said, 'so you noticed?'

His lips twisted. 'I notice everything about you, Liz Hillier. I always did. Hang on, let me guess.' He scanned her from head to toe but his gaze came back to rest on her face, her eyes particularly. 'It's a baby, isn't it?'

'It's a baby,' she agreed gravely.

He paused. 'How do you feel about that?' he asked slowly then.

'I'm over the moon.' She slipped her arms around his neck. 'Can I tell you why?'

'Of course...'

'I used to worry,' she said barely audibly, 'that I could never prove to you how much I loved you, I could only say it. But this is my proof. I want your baby with all my being.'

'Oh, Liz,' was all he said but she could see his heart in his eyes, and she knew that he really believed her.

He caught his breath as he saw the joy in her. 'Come,' he said, and she knew exactly what he had in mind.

They turned and walked away through the gardens to towards the house, hand in hand again.

JUNE 2011
HARDBACK TITLES

ROMANCE

Passion and the Prince	Penny Jordan
For Duty's Sake	Lucy Monroe
Alessandro's Prize	Helen Bianchin
Mr and Mischief	Kate Hewitt
Wife in the Shadows	Sara Craven
The Brooding Stranger	Maggie Cox
An Inconvenient Obsession	Natasha Tate
The Girl He Never Noticed	Lindsay Armstrong
The Privileged and the Damned	Kimberly Lang
The Big Bad Boss	Susan Stephens
Her Desert Prince	Rebecca Winters
A Family for the Rugged Rancher	Donna Alward
The Boss's Surprise Son	Teresa Carpenter
Soldier on Her Doorstep	Soraya Lane
Ordinary Girl in a Tiara	Jessica Hart
Tempted by Trouble	Liz Fielding
Flirting with the Society Doctor	Janice Lynn
When One Night Isn't Enough	Wendy S Marcus

HISTORICAL

Ravished by the Rake	Louise Allen
The Rake of Hollowhurst Castle	Elizabeth Beacon
Bought for the Harem	Anne Herries
Slave Princess	Juliet Landon

MEDICAL™

Melting the Argentine Doctor's Heart	Meredith Webber
Small Town Marriage Miracle	Jennifer Taylor
St Piran's: Prince on the Children's Ward	Sarah Morgan
Harry St Clair: Rogue or Doctor?	Fiona McArthur

JUNE 2011
LARGE PRINT TITLES

ROMANCE

Flora's Defiance	Lynne Graham
The Reluctant Duke	Carole Mortimer
The Wedding Charade	Melanie Milburne
The Devil Wears Kolovsky	Carol Marinelli
The Nanny and the CEO	Rebecca Winters
Friends to Forever	Nikki Logan
Three Weddings and a Baby	Fiona Harper
The Last Summer of Being Single	Nina Harrington

HISTORICAL

Lady Arabella's Scandalous Marriage	Carole Mortimer
Dangerous Lord, Seductive Miss	Mary Brendan
Bound to the Barbarian	Carol Townend
The Shy Duchess	Amanda McCabe

MEDICAL™

St Piran's: The Wedding of The Year	Caroline Anderson
St Piran's: Rescuing Pregnant Cinderella	Carol Marinelli
A Christmas Knight	Kate Hardy
The Nurse Who Saved Christmas	Janice Lynn
The Midwife's Christmas Miracle	Jennifer Taylor
The Doctor's Society Sweetheart	Lucy Clark

JULY 2011
HARDBACK TITLES

ROMANCE

The Marriage Betrayal	Lynne Graham
The Ice Prince	Sandra Marton
Doukakis's Apprentice	Sarah Morgan
Surrender to the Past	Carole Mortimer
Heart of the Desert	Carol Marinelli
Reckless Night in Rio	Jennie Lucas
Her Impossible Boss	Cathy Williams
The Replacement Wife	Caitlin Crews
Dating and Other Dangers	Natalie Anderson
The S Before Ex	Mira Lyn Kelly
Her Outback Commander	Margaret Way
A Kiss to Seal the Deal	Nikki Logan
Baby on the Ranch	Susan Meier
The Army Ranger's Return	Soraya Lane
Girl in a Vintage Dress	Nicola Marsh
Rapunzel in New York	Nikki Logan
The Doctor & the Runaway Heiress	Marion Lennox
The Surgeon She Never Forgot	Melanie Milburne

HISTORICAL

Seduced by the Scoundrel	Louise Allen
Unmasking the Duke's Mistress	Margaret McPhee
To Catch a Husband…	Sarah Mallory
The Highlander's Redemption	Marguerite Kaye

MEDICAL™

The Playboy of Harley Street	Anne Fraser
Doctor on the Red Carpet	Anne Fraser
Just One Last Night…	Amy Andrews
Suddenly Single Sophie	Leonie Knight

06011 Gen Std LP

JULY 2011
LARGE PRINT TITLES

ROMANCE

A Stormy Spanish Summer	Penny Jordan
Taming the Last St Claire	Carole Mortimer
Not a Marrying Man	Miranda Lee
The Far Side of Paradise	Robyn Donald
The Baby Swap Miracle	Caroline Anderson
Expecting Royal Twins!	Melissa McClone
To Dance with a Prince	Cara Colter
Molly Cooper's Dream Date	Barbara Hannay

HISTORICAL

Lady Folbroke's Delicious Deception	Christine Merrill
Breaking the Governess's Rules	Michelle Styles
Her Dark and Dangerous Lord	Anne Herries
How To Marry a Rake	Deb Marlowe

MEDICAL™

Sheikh, Children's Doctor...Husband	Meredith Webber
Six-Week Marriage Miracle	Jessica Matthews
Rescued by the Dreamy Doc	Amy Andrews
Navy Officer to Family Man	Emily Forbes
St Piran's: Italian Surgeon, Forbidden Bride	Margaret McDonagh
The Baby Who Stole the Doctor's Heart	Dianne Drake